Praise for *Ex...*

"*Expiration Date* is a skillful, fast-paced, ro...
story with believable characters and a pe...
line entertainment."

Praise for *Severance Package*

"A kinetic story, which never stops moving . . . turbocharged entertainment."
—Marilyn Stasio, *The New York Times*

"Swierczynski writes a brand of thriller whose pacing forces us to reexamine our casual use of the word *breakneck*. . . . This is essentially one long action scene that begs for the next Tarantino to direct. But if that sounds like faint praise, it isn't: there are both enough cliché killers and comedy to make us raise two thumbs up. If you want your thrillers to be, well, thrilling, pop a big bowl of corn—you won't leave your seat until the end."
—*Booklist*

"The best word to describe Swierczynski's latest thriller is *frenetic*, and even that is likely an understatement."
—*Library Journal*

"This action fest moves swiftly to its darkly satisfying conclusion."
—*Publishers Weekly*

"A guilty pleasure of unparalleled magnitude, with pedal-to-the-metal pacing, characters who appear to be meek cubicle dwellers à la *Office Space* but are really cold-blooded black-ops killers, and enough gut-churning violence to make a Quentin Tarantino movie look like a Disney musical replete with singing candlesticks and teapots. The dark, twisted energy in this novel is palpable."
—*Chicago Tribune*

"Wildly violent and way funny, the book's a summer blockbuster waiting to be filmed. Grade: A-."
—*Philadelphia* magazine

"Duane Swierczynski speeds through his action-filled plot, replete with bloodshed, mayhem, and twists. His prose draws the reader in, and his short chapters and revved-up action sequences make *Severance Package* a one-sitting read. . . . This novel is as powerful as an unexpected punch in the stomach."
—*The Omaha World-Herald* (Nebraska)

Praise for *The Blonde*

"Compulsively readable . . . rockets forward with inventive ferocity. [The] plot uncoils in a rapid-fire series of time-coded moments that generate a relentless tension. Brilliantly paced insanity."
—*Houston Chronicle*

"Two parts adrenaline rush, one part medical thriller, this twisted story starts with a bang and rarely slows down. Full of offbeat characters, excruciatingly reckless twists, and sardonic humor, this fun ride shows great promise for a rising author."
—*Library Journal* (starred review)

"This is delicious postmodern hard-boiled punk rock storytelling. Swierczynski's hit man character is as funny and fresh as he is fierce and quick. *The Blonde* is masterfully paced, wonderfully rendered, and devastatingly entertaining."
—Greg Rucka, Eisner Award–winning author of *Queen & Country* and
2006 Barry Award–nominated thriller *Private Wars*

"Duane Swierczynski's new novel, *The Blonde*, is as lean as a starving model, mean as a snake, and fast as a jet. It's also one hell of fine read. This guy has got to be the hottest new thing in crime fiction, and *The Blonde* is one of the best crime reads I've had in some time."　　　　　—Joe R. Lansdale, Edgar-winning author of *Sunset and Sawdust*

"Page-turning tension . . . a story so bizarre that it just might be true."　　—*Kirkus Reviews*

"A hilarious nail-biter, a tour-de-force by a young writer who has already carved out this unique take on the crime genre, so it's futile to compare it to anything else. . . . It is sui generis. It is perfect."　—Laura Lippman, bestselling author of *What the Dead Know*

"Another fast, funny, and action-packed outing from a writer who, fortunately for us, doesn't seem to know how to slow down."　　　　　　　　　—*Booklist*

"Quite a ride. The prose is hard-boiled enough to crack walnuts and the action more precipitous than a bobsled run."　　　　　　　—*The Philadelphia Inquirer*

"Mr. Swierczynski knows how to streamline a story, keep the pace breakneck, sucking all the oxygen out of the room while he tells you this very gritty and nervy story about a pickup gone wrong. Delicious dialogue, funny realizations, and one hell of a ride."
　　　　　　　　　　　　　　　　—Frank Bascombe, *Ain't It Cool News*

Praise for *The Wheelman*

"If you are partial to fast-paced thrillers that present this world as an unforgiving, blood-soaked wasteland, you should love Duane Swierczynski's first novel. Swierczynski's novel, like those of [Elmore] Leonard, offers an undertow of humor beneath the churning sea of man's inhumanity."　　　　　　　—*The Washington Post*

"Swierczynski has an uncommon gift for the banal lunacy of criminal dialogue, a delightfully devious eye for character, and a surprisingly well-developed narrative for a beginner."　　　　　　　　　　　　　—*Chicago Tribune*

"Adrenaline-charged . . . fast-moving and funny, *The Wheelman* is Mr. Toad's Wild Ride in an R-rated amusement park."　　　　　　　　　—*Booklist*

"I canceled a night out and stayed up all night reading. That's how much I loved this book . . . at every turn, I was blindsided. Hilarious and bloody violent."
　　　　　　　—Ken Bruen, author of the Shamus Award–winning *The Guards*

"A great heist story in the rich tradition of Richard Stark's Parker novels and Stanley Kubrick's *The Killing* . . . keeps readers holding their breath to see what's going to happen next. It is clearly the work of a maturing writer who is possessed of a keen style and abundant talent."　　　　　　　　　—*The Philadelphia Inquirer*

"Dark stuff . . . hilariously funny at the same time. Swierczynski has come up with his own twisted and thoroughly enjoyable genre. Bring on some more, sir."
　　　　　　　　　　　　　　　　　　　—*Rocky Mountain News*

"Oh, what style!"　　　　　　　　　　　　　　　—*Kirkus Reviews*

EXPIRATION DATE

WIERCZYNSKI

ALSO BY DUANE SWIERCZYNSKI

NOVELS
SECRET DEAD MEN
THE WHEELMAN
THE BLONDE
SEVERANCE PACKAGE

INTERACTIVE MYSTERIES
THE CRIMES OF DR. WATSON
BATMAN: MURDER AT WAYNE MANOR

GRAPHIC NOVELS
CABLE: WAR BABY
CABLE: WAITING FOR THE END OF THE WORLD
IMMORTAL IRON FIST: THE MORTAL IRON FIST
IMMORTAL IRON FIST: ESCAPE FROM THE EIGHTH CITY
WEREWOLF BY NIGHT: IN THE BLOOD
THE PUNISHER: SIX HOURS TO KILL

AS EDITOR
DAMN NEAR DEAD

EXPIRATION DATE

DUANE SWIERCZYNSKI

 MINOTAUR BOOKS ≋ NEW YORK

FOR

LOUIS WOJCIECHOWSKI

1926–2009

This is a work of fiction. All of the characters, organizations, and events portrayed in this novel are either products of the author's imagination or are used fictitiously.

Book design by Greg Collins.

www.minotaurbooks.com

Library of Congress Cataloging-in-Publication Data

Swierczynski, Duane.
    Expiration date / Duane Swierczynski. — 1st ed.
        p. cm.
    ISBN 978-0-312-36340-6
    1. Private investigators—Pennsylvania—Philadelphia—Fiction. 2. Time travel—Fiction. 3. Murder—Investigation—Fiction. I. Title.
    PS3619.W53E97 2010
    813'.6—dc22

                                                                        2009039947

First Edition: April 2010

10 9 8 7 6 5 4 3 2 1

WELL—
SO IT GOES:
TIME HITS THE HARDEST BLOWS.

—JOSEPH MONCURE MARCH

SEE THAT BODY SPRAWLED on the hardwood floor, marinating in a pool of his own blood?

That's me.

Five minutes ago I was shot in the back. Three times, right between the shoulder blades. The guy who runs the late-night beer bodega downstairs, Willie Shahid, heard the shots—*bang bang bang*—then saw somebody with a revolver go shuffling down Frankford Avenue. After a few minutes, he walked upstairs to check it out.

Now Willie's outside the apartment door. He knocks, and then waits a second. Something's not right. He sniffs the air; the acrid scent of chalk and burnt paper fills his nostrils. *Gunpowder.* It's not an unfamiliar scent to Willie Shahid. Not in this neighborhood.

Watch Willie Shahid take out his cell and dial 911, giving the proper address and even the floor. Guy's a real pro.

If you hang around a little longer, you'll see the EMTs arrive, and then the Philly PD, 15th District. They'll move me to a stretcher and carry me out the front door of the building, under the rumbling El train and past a bunch of dudes in oversized white T-shirts and deadpan expressions.

Soon the surgeons at nearby Frankford Hospital will dig the slugs out of my back, place them in a kidney-shaped steel tray. From there, they'll transfer them to a plastic evidence bag and send it down to the Philadelphia Police Department's forensics lab at Eighth and Race. Standard procedure—bullets from GSWs always go right to the lab for ballistic analysis.

A few days later confusion will sweep over the forensics guys' faces. Identifying the type of bullet will be no problem: .38 caliber.

No, something else will trouble them.

After analyzing the slugs and gunpowder, the CSI guys will determine that the bullets are at least forty years old. They'll also discover that this specific type stopped being manufactured back in 1967.

Now, old bullets can still work. But they'll have to be asking themselves: Why use forty-year-old ammunition to snuff somebody?

SOME PEOPLE HAVE THE idea that when you die your life flashes before your eyes, like a movie on fast-forward.

Not quite.

Time's arrow only appears to fly straight when you're alive. Dead is something else. Once you cross that invisible line, you see things how they really are. You see that every moment seems to happen all at once.

Which makes telling this story—or the most important parts of it, anyway—difficult. Usually, you start at the beginning. Or the middle, so the listener doesn't get bored.

Problem is, I'm very hazy on the beginning and the middle, as I came in during the end. I can speculate, but it'd be nothing more than a wild guess.

I guess I should start with the day I moved into the apartment and went back in time.

I

THOMAS JEFFERSON GOES TO A PORNO

I WAS SITTING ON MY front stoop, drinking a Sierra Nevada Pale Ale. At eleven bucks a six-pack, Sierra's a splurge beer, so I tried to savor every sip. I'd probably be drinking pounder cans of Pabst Blue Ribbon from now on.

After a while Meghan came out and I handed her the last one. She thanked me by bumping shoulders. We sat for a while and drank our beers in the warm downtown sun. It would have been a perfect day if I wasn't moving out.

Meghan leaned back on her elbows, blond hair hanging down across her forehead.

"You sure I can't give you a ride?"

I swallowed, enjoying the bitter taste of hops in my mouth, the bright sun on my face. Then I looked at her.

"Frankford's kind of a bad neighborhood."

"No neighborhoods are bad, Mickey. They're just misunderstood."

"No, seriously. It's bad. There was a story in yesterday's *Daily News*. Some high school kid there was murdered by three of his friends. And I don't mean over a dumb fight over sneakers or drugs. I mean, they planned his execution, killed him, then worked hard to hide the evidence."

"They didn't work too hard if the *Daily News* found out about it."

Meghan and I had been friends since the year before, when I moved to Sixteenth and Spruce, just a few blocks away from swank Rittenhouse Square. If you've ever been to Philadelphia, you know the square I'm talking about—high-end restaurants, high-rise condos. I couldn't afford this neighborhood even when I was gainfully employed.

But two weeks ago my alt-weekly newspaper, the *Philadelphia City Press*, decided they could get by with only one staff writer. They wished me all the best. Since no other papers were crying out for my services, here or elsewhere, I joined the ranks of the newly unemployed. Just like hundreds of thousands of other people.

So now my meager possessions were almost packed and I was waiting for a ride from my mom so she could take me to my grandfather's cramped—yet rent-free—efficiency in Frankford, which was a long, long way from Rittenhouse Square.

Normally I refused to accept any help or advice from my mom. The less she knew about my life, the less I owed her, the better. But my back was up against the wall now. I couldn't afford another week in this apartment, let alone another month. I had no money for a deposit on another apartment.

I was moving back to Frankford.

Slumming is one thing when you're twenty-two and just out of college and backed up by a deep-pile parental checking account. But moving to a bad neighborhood when you're thirty-seven and have exhausted all other options is something else entirely. It's a heavy thing with a rope, dragging you down to a lower social depth with no easy way back to the surface.

Worst of all, you can still see them up there—the friends you graduated with fifteen years ago—laughing and splashing around, having a good time.

The last thing I wanted was Meghan to escort me to the bottom of the ocean, give me an awkward hug, then swim back up to the party. She'd offered to drive me at least a half-dozen times over the past two weeks, and I repeatedly had told her no, my mom insisted on taking me.

Which was a total friggin' lie.

"You don't want to go to Frankford," I said. "It's one of the busiest drug corridors in the city. It even used to have its own serial killer."

"Now you're just making stuff up."

"Completely serious. Happened when I was in high school—in the late 1980s. The guy was called the Frankford Slasher, and he killed a bunch of prostitutes. I wrote a piece about it for the *Press*."

"That was Jack the Ripper."

"It was also the Frankford Slasher."

"Still think you're making it up."

I pushed myself up by pressing my palms on the warm brownstone.

"I'd better finish packing. A couple of teenagers could be plotting my death as we speak, and I don't want to disappoint them."

"Or the Frankford Slasher."

"Fortunately, I'm not a prostitute."

"Not yet."

"Nice."

There was an awkward moment of silence. Then Meghan looked at me.

"Call your mom, Mickey. Tell her I'm driving you."

FRANKFORD WASN'T ALWAYS A bad neighborhood. A couple hundred years ago it was a nice quiet village where the framers of the Constitution would spend their summers to escape the stifling heat of the city. I could show you the place—Womrath Park—where Thomas Jefferson allegedly kicked back and read the Declaration of Independence for the first time in public.

But take Thomas Jefferson to Womrath Park now. Introduce him to the new owners of the park—the hard young men selling little white chunks of smokeable *snuff*. Walk him into the triple-X theater across the street, where he'd be treated to projected images of people engaged in a very different sort of *congress*.

You could almost imagine him marching back down to Independence Hall and saying: *Look, fellas, I think we oughta think this whole "freedom" thing through a bit more.*

A century after Jefferson, Frankford the Quiet Country Village morphed into Frankford the Bustling Industrial Neighborhood. It was a popular way station on the road (King's Highway) from Philadelphia to New York City. The streets were crowded with factories and mills, along with modest-but-sturdy rowhomes for the workers who labored in them. There were cotton mills, bleacheries, wool mills, iron works and calico print works. There was a bustling arsenal and gunpowder mill. The industry thrived for a while, then sputtered, then died. Just like it did in the rest of the country.

But they say the neighborhood was truly doomed in 1922, the year the city ran an elevated train down its main artery—Frankford Avenue—shrouding the shops below in darkness and pigeon crap. White flight to the suburbs began in the 1950s. Then, in the 1960s, drugs found Frankford, and invited all of its friends to stay.

And I'd told Meghan the truth: a serial killer really did prowl the dark avenue under the El, late at night, looking for drunks and prostitutes in the 1980s around dive bars like Brady's at Bridge and Pratt. The Slasher was never caught.

A Philly band called American Dream had a minor pop hit back in the early 1970s called "Frankford El." The chorus explained that you can't get to Heaven on the Frankford El. Why?

Because the Frankford El goes straight to . . . Frankford.

GRANDPOP'S BLOCK LOOKED LIKE a junkie's smile. Starting from the extreme left, you had the dirty concrete steps leading up to the Margaret Street station of the El. Right next door, an abandoned building. Then, a weeded lot. A three-story building. Weeded lot. Grandpop's building, the ground floor occupied by one of those beer/rolling paper/pork rind bodegas that upset City Council so much. Weeded lot. Weeded lot.

Out of an original eight buildings on this strip of Frankford Avenue, only three remained.

My new place was up on the third floor, where it appeared I'd have an excellent view of the El tracks.

Meghan gazed up at the dirty underbelly of the El through her windshield. Pigeons nested around up there, covering every possible square inch with their chunky white shit.

"It's not so bad."

"You're right. If you squint, it's eerily reminiscent of Rittenhouse Square."

"This is probably the next great undiscovered neighborhood. Look what they did to Fishtown and Northern Liberties."

"Yeah. They could level the area with a bunker buster and start all over."

She scanned the block. Across the street was a rusty metal kiosk that, if I remember correctly, used to be a newsstand. Now it appeared to be a community urinal.

"Think it's okay to park here?"

Meghan was born and raised on Philadelphia's so-called Main

Line. You remember the movie—Cary Grant, Katharine Hepburn, all that? That's the Main Line. I remembered watching the movie on TV as a kid and wondering why they called it *The Philadelphia Story*, because they certainly couldn't have filmed it in Philadelphia.

The Philly I knew was *Rocky, Twelve Monkeys.* Hardcore gritty tales set in unforgiving concrete canyons. Meghan claimed to love the rough-and-tumble Philadelphia from *Rocky* and *Twelve Monkeys.* I had to gently remind her that the latter was a postapocalyptic film.

Still, I couldn't blame her.

She didn't grow up here.

WHEN I LEFT FRANKFORD after college I swore I'd never return. You get punched in the face often enough, chased down the block and through your own front door often enough . . . well, it kind of puts you off a neighborhood.

As a kid, I mostly stayed in my back bedroom and read whatever I could get my hands on. And later, I wrote stories. Looking back on it now, it seems I was plotting my escape all along, because it was a writing career that got me out of Frankford.

And now, the lack of a writing career was bringing me back.

My mom had come up with the idea of me crashing here until I found another job. It wasn't like Grandpop Henry would know the difference. The downstairs bodega owner had found him a few hours after he'd suffered some kind of seizure and fell into a coma—the same day I lost my job at the *City Press*, in fact. Not exactly a banner day for the family.

My mom told me that Grandpop Henry could breathe on his own. But now he was like a TV without cable: the power was on, only he couldn't receive any programming.

"You should still visit him. He can still hear you."

"Okay."

"He'll only be a few blocks away."

"Okay."

"You're going to visit him, right?"

"Okay."

My mother delighted in telling me what to do, and I found a not too small measure of satisfaction doing the exact opposite.

She also told me that Grandpop's apartment was fully furnished, so I wouldn't have to worry about pots, pans or utensils. Not that I owned much of that stuff. My worldly possessions included a crate of old LPs from the 1960s and 70s; a box of Hunter S. Thompson and Charles Bukowski paperbacks—standard issue for journalists; another box of vintage paperback mysteries; a six-year-old Mac laptop; a three-year-old cell phone that didn't close right; and finally, two trash bags full of clothes and other assorted junk I've been dragging around for fifteen years, from Philly to New York City and back.

It's sad when your worldly possessions fit into a 2009 Toyota Prius.

On the upside, we finished unloading in less than thirty minutes, even though it was three flights up to Apartment 3-A. I drove Meghan's Prius to the Frankford Hospital garage a few blocks away, where I assumed it would be reasonably safe. After all, doctors parked there, right?

Meghan gave me a playful punch in the arm.

"So, what now?"

"Well, I was about to have my boy Tino mix me a gin gimlet before retiring to the terrace to watch the sunset."

"Send Tino home for the night. Let's get drunk on beer."

"Excellent suggestion. But I'll have to go get your car again."

"What, and drive back wasted? Let's go downstairs and buy a few sixes."

"Downstairs?"

"The bodega. They sell beer. I saw the signs in the window and everything."

So we walked downstairs to the bodega. I bought two sixes from Willie Shahid—though I didn't know his name yet. Meghan looked like she was having a grand old time, buying beer in Frankford. Meanwhile, I worried some crackhead in a ski mask was going to pop in, wave a gun around and ask for the keys to the late-model Prius parked in the hospital garage up the street.

I was also mildly alarmed when the tab for two sixes of Yuengling came to $18, leaving me with about five bucks until my final paycheck was direct deposited the next day. But hey, the lady wanted to get her beer on. Tonight, money was no object.

Tonight, we were toasting my sad return home.

ABOUT AN HOUR LATER I'd killed four of the Yuenglings and lined the empties up on top of Grandpop Henry's massive cherrywood desk. Meghan, first beer still in hand, was on the floor going through his stuff without shyness or apology.

"I'm a snoop."

There wasn't much to Apartment 3-A—just a big room with a bathroom off to one side, a small closet on the other. A rusty radiator in the corner for all your heating needs. A desktop circulating fan for cooling, which would do jack shit once summer really got under way. A small kitchenette with a miniature oven barely big enough for a TV dinner and a quarter-sized fridge that could accommodate beer or food, but not both at the same time.

Grandpop Henry moved here in 2002, but I'd never visited. I feel a little guilty about that—but then again, I also didn't go out of my way to return to Frankford either.

Every few minutes the thunder of the Frankford El smashed through the silence, and through the dirty front windows you could see the rushing silver of the train cars as they ground to a halt at the Margaret Street station, then, after a ten-second delay, started moving again, and the rumble would build to a deafening crescendo that bounced off the fronts of the buildings all the way down to the next station.

The place was reasonably clean—no nicotine buildup on the walls, no grease caked on the ceiling of the kitchenette. Grandpop Henry, it seemed, owned only two pieces of furniture: a big houndstooth couch and the big cherrywood desk. No bed, no kitchen table, no chairs. Guess when it comes down to it, all you needed was something to sit on and something to put things on.

Still, the room was cluttered, a ridiculous amount of floor space devoted to cardboard boxes, plastic milk crates and shoe boxes crammed with papers. This was what Meghan picked through.

"What does your grandfather do for a living?"

"He's retired. But he used to be a night watchman at a hospital. My mom told me he liked the hours, the lack of conscious people."

"Huh."

"What's the *huh* for?"

"He's got a lot of papers here. Newspaper clippings, genealogy charts, handwritten notes. A lot of medical reports, it looks like. I thought maybe he was a journalist or something. Like you."

"My grandpop? I don't think he was much of a reader."

"Hmmm."

After a while Meghan showed me a yellowed envelope.

"Henryk Wadcheck?"

She mispronounced it the way most people do: *wad-chek*. As in, check your wad. The kids in grade school figured it out pretty quick.

"My grandfather's name. It's Polish. And pronounced *vahd*-chek."

"My, that's *veeeered*. So wait—is that your last name?"

"Technically."

"Your name is Mickey Wadcheck? How did I not know this?"

"My dad played music under the name Anthony Wade. So I adopted Wade for my byline. You would, too, if you had a name like *vahd-chek*."

Meghan smiled.

"You know I'm totally calling you Mr. Wadcheck from now on."

"Please don't."

Bad enough I have "Mickey" for a handle. The name on my birth certificate is "Mick," in honor of Messrs. Jagger and Ronson, two of my dad's musician heroes. You can't call a five-year-old "Mick," of course, so it soon became "Mickey." And my classmates right away thought of the mouse. My childhood was full of *M-I-C (see you real soon . . . gaywad!)* jokes, not to mention that horrible stretch in 1982 when Toni Basil totally friggin' ruined my life. I was ten, and I swore a blood oath to crush the skull of the next person to tell me *I was so fine, so fine I blew their mind.* The only person who had it worse that year was a classmate named Eileen, who didn't understand why her leering male classmates were suddenly talking about *coming on her.*

"Oh my God—will you look at this."

Meghan crawled over and handed me a photo of a man in a WWII-era military uniform. My grandpop.

"He looks just like you, Mr. Wadcheck!"

"Don't call me that. And yeah, I've been told there's a resemblance, but I don't see it. Maybe if you saw him in person . . ."

"Bah. You're a dead ringer."

I twisted open another Yuengling as Meghan picked through another box, sitting on the floor, legs crossed, shoeless. I liked the way her blond hair dangled in front of her face and it didn't seem to bother her in the least.

"Did you two used to spend a lot of time together?"

"Not really. Grandpop Henry's always been a little weird. Kind of gruff, spare-the-rod-spoil-the-child kind of guy. Imagine Walter Matthau in *Grumpy Old Men*."

"I thought you two might be close, considering . . ."

She left that hanging midair, waiting for me to finish: *what had happened to my father.*

Late one night at McGillin's Ale House, the oldest continuously operating bar in Philly, I'd told her about what had happened to my dad. She didn't press, I didn't elaborate. It had never come up again, until now.

I took another pull from my beer.

"Yeah, well, no. I see my grandmother a lot."

"Define *a lot*."

"Holidays? I see her for at least one or two of the important ones."

"Thought as much. So they're divorced?"

"A long time ago. My dad was ten or eleven, I think."

I regretted bringing my dad up, because whenever I thought about him with alcohol in my system, I started getting pissed off and morose. And I didn't want to be pissed off or morose in front of Meghan.

I tried to lighten the mood.

"So to recap: I'm jobless. I live in a bad neighborhood. And I don't have much in the way of male role models."

Meghan smiled, leaning up and touching my face. I loved the feel of her fingertips. They were cool and warm at the same time.

"And yet, you're such a gentleman, Mr. Wadcheck."

"Please don't call me Mr. Wadcheck."

We sat there together, pretty much easygoing quiet, for another hour or so. I finished two more beers and wondered how long I'd

be stuck in this dump. This time Meghan and I were enjoying together was unlikely to happen again. I wouldn't ask her to drive to
Frankford again. Not in a million years.

So if I wanted to hang out with her again I'd have to take the El
back down to Rittenhouse Square. And until I found a job, I
couldn't see myself doing that. What was I going to do, buy her a
dog and ask her to sit with me by the little bronze goat in the park?

A few minutes before midnight, just as I was really starting to
dread the idea of walking Meghan down Frankford Avenue back
to her car, she blindsided me.

"Hey, you mind if I crash here for the night?"

My stomach did a happy little flip. But I played it cool.

"Yeah, sure. I mean, no, I don't mind. That would be great. Really great."

I was so smooth it sometimes hurt.

THERE WAS NO BED—just the scratchy houndstooth couch, which
Meghan discovered was a pullout. I prayed for clean sheets; God,
for once, heard my plea. Meghan wrestled a fitted sheet onto the
wafer-thin mattress as I tugged some cases over pillows.

"Good night," I told Meghan's shape.

"Goot night, Meester Vahhhdcheck."

"You're hilarious."

"Vyyy know."

We settled in for sleep. Well, she did, anyway.

I sat up and watched her for a while. Her lips were parted
slightly, long blond hair fanning the lumpy pillow—a perfect vision
of peace. Then again, Meghan seems at ease in any given environ-
ment. Put her in a prix fixe Walnut Street restaurant or a South
Street dive on PBR and Jack night. She belongs, either way.

And she can pretty much float in and out of any situation she wants. Once I asked her what she did for a living, and she told me she was "deferring life." Meghan can do this because she is the youngest daughter of a powerful Center City lawyer.

I, on the other hand, am the son of a dead hippie musician, and I feel out of place pretty much everywhere. Even people in dives don't seem too sure about me. I believe that was either my saving grace as a reporter, or my undoing. John Gregory Dunne once wrote that reporters were supposed to feel like outcasts, hands and noses pressed up against the glass, watching the party on the other side. Sounded about right to me.

Nothing has ever happened between me and Meghan, a state of affairs that seems likely to continue the rest of our natural lives. I belong on the other side of the glass. I am supposed to be content to know that a woman like Meghan exists.

But why had she insisted on giving me a ride? Was this a good-bye visit? Was she just bored? Or maybe . . .

Maybe it was nothing at all.

A FEW HOURS LATER my eyes popped open, my head pounding. Probably a combination of too many beers and no food. I tossed. I turned. The humidity in the apartment was thick as an afghan blanket. Once in a while I'd glance over at Meghan. She still looked perfect.

I rolled out of bed and padded my way to the bathroom mirror, where I was confronted by a sweaty, disheveled thirty-seven-year-old who looked like he needed a nap and a hug. I splashed water over his face, cupped some into his mouth and urged him to spit.

Grandpop Henry's bathroom was strictly no frills—just a shower stall with an opaque glass door, sink and medicine cabinet.

Black-and-white-checkered tile on the floor, framed photograph of a fishing boat above the toilet. An old man's bathroom.

I dried my face, opened the medicine cabinet door. Something banged against the wall. I pulled the door back a few inches. A metal clasp had been mounted on it. And on top of the toilet tank was an open rusty padlock. Did Grandpop actually padlock his medicine cabinet shut at night? In case what—junkies broke in and stole his denture cream?

I found an oversized vintage jar of Tylenol with a worn and cracked label. Old people never throw anything away. I glanced at the expiration date: September 1982. Not exactly promising. Wasn't that the time around the whole tampering scare? I remember being ten years old and my mother throwing away every medicine bottle in the house, Tylenol brand or otherwise.

But the pills inside looked okay. It was entirely possible—likely, even—that my grandpop just used the same oversized plastic bottle and replenished the pills whenever he ran out. So I tapped four into my palm. They looked like 250-milligram tablets; a thousand sounded right. A few pain relievers in the middle of the night goes a long way toward easing a morning hangover.

I swallowed them, scooped more water into my mouth, swirled for a second, then spit. Chances were slim that Meghan would wake up and decide to make out with me, but I didn't want my mouth tasting like a bar sink, just in case.

I went back to bed, slid in next to Meghan and tucked my left arm under my pillow. She was in a deep sleep. I was tired, too. Long day.

I nodded off for a second and then woke up in someone else's room.

II

GOOD AS DEAD

I **WAS ON A COLD** hardwood floor. No sofa bed, no blanket, no pillow.

No Meghan.

The room looked like my grandpop's apartment, only someone had redecorated the place while I'd been sleeping. The front windows were covered with brown cardboard and masking tape. Tiny needles of light from the El station outside shot out from between the cracks. It was dark in here, but I could make out framed photos on the walls, and in the corner, a potted fern. All of the clutter—the boxes, the milk crates—was gone.

I heard the sound of groaning wood and turned to see a dark-haired woman, about my age, maybe a little older, sitting on a sofa behind me. She didn't seem to notice me. She was pretty, but had tired eyes, and wore a dress with little multicolored dots that look like they jumped off a bag of Wonder Bread.

"Uh, hi," I said.

She started speaking without making eye contact.

"You need a break. Come out with me. Have an old-fashioned. My treat."

"Excuse me?"

She used her palms to smooth out her Wonder Bread dress, then stood up and walked right by me. Like I wasn't even there.

I pushed myself up off the floor, trying to figure out what the hell was going on. Had I been sleepwalking? Did I wander into someone else's apartment on a different floor? The layout of this room was identical to my grandpop's apartment. Maybe I was in 2-A, or something. Of course, I had no idea how I might have pulled off such a trick.

Across the room the Wonder Bread Woman picked up a pack of Lucky Strikes from the top of my grandpop's polished wooden desk. It looked like the same desk on which I'd lined up my empties a short while ago. Only now there was a big guy sitting behind the desk—a seriously big guy. He wore a wrinkled white shirt, and the sleeves were rolled up, revealing forearm hair thick enough to catch flies.

The woman shook a cigarette loose, clicked open a metal snap lighter, puffed the cigarette to life.

The big guy sighed.

"I still need to type up these reports and I have someone coming by shortly for a session," he said.

"You work too many nights, Mitchell," the woman said.

"I have to. It's part of the exp— . . . job."

"There are more interesting ways to spend the night than talking to boring patients about their dreams. You could, for instance, be talking to me."

There was an awkward silence. Awkward for me, mostly. The fat guy behind the desk—Mitchell—finally broke it.

"Look, you should go downstairs to your boy, Erna. Feed him some dinner. It's late. He's probably starving."

"The boy's fine," she said. "He knows how to open a can."

Mitchell sighed and sat back in his chair. The floorboards creaked under his weight.

"Erna, sometimes I wonder if it was a mistake to let you have an apartment here."

"Admit it. You love having me around."

"Not when I have work to do."

OKAY, WHATEVER WAS GOING on here, it was none of my business, and I should get the hell out. I took a few cautious steps toward the desk.

"Hey, yeah," I said. "Look—Mitchell? Erna? I'm really sorry, guys. I don't know what happened, but I'll show myself out, okay?"

They didn't seem to hear me.

They didn't react to me at all.

"Come on, Mitchell, don't be a square your whole life," Erna said. "Just one old-fashioned at Brady's. Or maybe a beer. It's quitting time. I want to have a little fuuuuuun."

"It's Tuesday night," Mitchell said, "and you should be going home to bed."

"You always say that. And you never join me."

"Stop it. You should really check on your boy."

I was beginning to get a little freaked out so I started waving my arms.

"Uh . . . Yo! Over here. Can you people really not see me, or are you just screwing around?"

"Stop worrying about the boy," Erna said. "You're always telling me what to do with him. You act like he's yours sometimes."

"No, I don't. I'm not good with kids."

"I'm not asking you to be. Which is why he's downstairs and I'm asking you out for a drink."

Erna took a final drag from her cigarette, then blew the smoke out long and slow before mashing the butt in a glass ashtray on Mitchell's desk. I noticed a black nameplate on a brass holder: DR. MITCHELL DeMEO. Doctor, huh? I checked the rest of the room. There were two filing cabinets shoved up against one wall.

Then I realized this wasn't an apartment; this was an office. How the hell did I end up in a doctor's office?

Erna turned and walked past me, the rough fabric of her dress brushing against my bare arm. She sat back down on the couch, which was more of a high-backed lounge chair, all dark wood and maroon cushions. Her polka-dot dress flowed around her. She turned her feet inward and stared off into nothing. She was pouting.

"You never want to do anything fun," she said.

With nothing else to do, I sat down next to her. Maybe one of these two crackheads would notice me then. My limbs felt impossibly heavy, as if invisible weights had been strapped to my wrists and ankles. I needed a minute to think. I turned to Erna and drilled my eyes into the side of her head.

"So, just to be clear," I said, "you can't hear a thing I'm saying, can you?"

Erna said nothing.

"Not one thing."

Erna said nothing.

"Like I'm not even here."

Still nothing.

"I've got this rash on my testicles that, I swear, is brighter than those red dots on your dress."

Still nothing.

"Okay then. Just wanted to have it straight."

I might have been invisible to her, but I could smell her perfume, which was sweet and pungent. Her lips were open slightly, like she wanted to say something but was holding back. Outside, the El train cars rumbled down their tracks, vibrating the floor-boards beneath our feet. I could hear them screech to a halt, the doors thump open, and after a short while, close again. This all felt real. *I* felt real. Why couldn't these people see me?

"Come on, Mitchell, don't be an asshole. I'm not asking you to abandon your work. I'm just asking for one little drink."

"Erna, please. Not tonight."

She sighed, stood up, then padded softly across the room until she was standing next to Mitchell. Then she dropped to her knees. Mitchell pretended not to notice, but he was a bad actor. His eyes flicked to the left. On the floor, Erna tugged at his belt. It wouldn't come loose. She tugged again.

"*Erna.* You don't have to do this . . ."

"Ah, there we go. You're too tense. You need to relax."

There was the soft metal purr of a zipper, and then Erna's head disappeared behind the desk. Mitchell let his oversized head fall back, mouth open in a fat *O*, and all of a sudden I really didn't want to be here.

I darted across the room, averting my eyes, wishing I could turn off my ears so I wouldn't hear the slurping.

Now that I was seeing it up close, the door also had a piece of cardboard taped over one panel of pebbled glass. I reached for the knob. It was slippery. I tried to turn it quietly, but I couldn't seem to maintain a hold on the bastard.

There was more slurping, more moaning.

I forgot about being stealthy. I grabbed the knob hard, like I wanted to crush it, and gave it a cruel twist to the right. Behind me a moan turned into an *oh that's right momma that's right.* The door latch clicked. The door opened with a creak.

"Wh-whoa . . . what was that?"

"Nothing, Mitchell. Just relax."

The door went *clack* behind me. I looked down the hallway, which was dark but clean. The walls were gray and peeling. The threadbare carpet was gray, too, with faded pink floral designs blended into the fabric. Which was weird, because when I moved in earlier today the walls were painted off-white and the bare floor was covered in grime and dust. This was not the hallway I'd walked through earlier today. None of this made any sense whatsoever.

On the second-floor landing there were three doors leading to other apartments. As I walked by, the door to 2-C opened a crack. A sleepy-eyed boy of about twelve, with a shock of unruly red hair and wearing oddly old-fashioned footie pajamas, peeked out at me.

"Who are you?" he asked.

"I'm nobody," I said. "Go back to sleep."

"Did you come from the doctor's office? Is my mom up there?"

Oh God. His mother was Erna. I didn't want to be the one to tell him that yeah, his mother was upstairs, but she was a little busy at the moment. Then I realized something.

"Wait," I said. "You can *see* me, can't you?"

The kid narrowed his eyes skeptically.

"Are you one of the doc's patients?"

"No. I just moved in."

"Moved in where?"

"Upstairs."

"Nobody lives upstairs. Nobody except the doctor. And he doesn't even live there. That's his office. Who are you?"

"What I am is really confused and lost and I'm starting to think this is one long, weird-ass dream. What do you think? Do you think we're both dreaming right now?"

His eyes went wide. He quickly slammed the door shut.

Okay. So to recap: I wasn't totally invisible. I was in the correct apartment building.

Only, I wasn't.

I needed some fresh air. Maybe that would wake me up. Maybe I could walk downstairs to that beer bodega and have a nice cold one while I waited for consciousness to return. That would be a nice way to pass the rest of a dream, right?

I stepped outside the front door, expecting a sticky wave of early June humidity. Instead, a gust of icy air sliced through my body. Jesus Christ, did the temperature just drop sixty degrees?

Then I looked down Frankford Avenue. It took my brain a few seconds to register what I was seeing.

CARS.

Very, very old cars.

FRANKFORD AVENUE WAS LINED with them Buicks, Cadillacs, Dodges, Fords, Pontiacs. All of them vintage autos you don't see outside of 1970s crime flicks. Giant slabs of American-made steel. It was as if someone had moved all of the normal cars off the street in preparation for a 1970s muscle car show. Which didn't make sense. If you were throwing a vintage auto show, you weren't going to throw it under the El.

Another cannon blast of freezing air cut through my body so hard my eyes teared up. I'd never had a dream this vivid before.

This was still Frankford Avenue—sort of. The El was still up above me, but the framework was the old green metal one they tore down in the late 1980s. The store windows were naked—not a single metal security shutter in sight. And the stores were all different. Candy shops and children's clothing emporiums and nonchain drugstores, with hand-painted paper sale signs advertising new products and sale prices taped to the windows.

More jarring was the fact that my grandpop's block was no longer a broken smile. All eight buildings were there, constituting a full block. There was a diner. A lingerie shop. The old original El station, with the pizza stand on the ground floor. The bodega on the ground floor was gone; instead, it was an old-fashioned delicatessen.

This was a dream, then. I was dreaming about the Frankford I knew as a kid.

But these weren't hazy, sun-baked Polaroid childhood memories. This was Frankford after dark, and when I was a kid I was never allowed out on the streets of Frankford this late at night.

I thought about going back inside, finding some dream clothes in an imaginary closet somewhere and coming back out to explore. But even though I was shivering, I couldn't resist the urge to go exploring right now.

I walked around in a daze. Frankford Avenue looked more cramped then I remembered, the El not quite as high above me. There were no empty storefronts. There was very little graffiti. This was like a movie set Frankford, built to approximate what it must have looked like in happier times. Was I remembering all of this with any degree of accuracy? Or was I making all of this shit up?

Somewhere around Church Street, about ten blocks away, I felt something whip around my leg—a sheet of newspaper. My eyes were drawn to the headlines first, but the headlines made no sense:

SAIGON ENDORSES NIXON'S VISIT TO CHINA

I glanced at the old-timey font on the top of the paper, expecting it to read *The Philadelphia Inquirer.*

But instead it was *The Evening Bulletin,* a newspaper that had been shuttered for close to thirty years now. In the right-hand corner, a black box told me I was holding the four-star sports edition. The cover price was twenty-five cents.

The date: *February 22, 1972.*

Which happened to be the day I was born.

THE NIGHT SKY TURNED a shade brighter, as if God suddenly remembered *shit, yeah, morning, better flick the dimmer switch up a little.* A dizziness washed over me like I'd been mainlining tequila.

There were more people out now, rushing past me, and they couldn't see me—the shivering guy in T-shirt and gym shorts on a freezing morning in late February 1972. They were working-class Frankford people, in coveralls and slacks and dresses, making their way from their rowhomes and apartments to the El station for their daily commute. I wondered what downtown Philly looked like now, in this dream 1972. Maybe I should follow the crowd, hop on the El with them, check the city out. Look at the skyline in the time before they broke the City Hall height barrier.

But then another head rush hit me. My skin started to itch and burn. I decided to skip my trip down to dream Center City and go back to the apartment . . . the office . . . whatever. Maybe Erna was done blowing Mitchell by now. Maybe I could lay down on that stiff-looking sofa and then wake up back in bed with Meghan. I could question the mechanics later.

My skin was really burning now. I started to worry a little. I didn't want to dream about burning to death on Frankford Avenue only to wake up with a space heater knocked over on top of me and discover, *wow, I've actually burned to death.* Cue Rod Serling.

I raced down the avenue, weaving in and around people who

couldn't see me. Only one dude, pushing a broom in front of his corner drugstore, seemed to follow me with his eyes.

By the time I reached the third floor of Grandpop Henry's building I was having serious head rushes. Usually one head rush was enough to make you slow down, but these kept coming. I needed to lie down. Or wake up. Or something. I reached for the doorknob.

It was locked.

I tugged at it, then remembered. It had self-locked when I'd left.

Wait, what was I talking about? This was a goddamned dream, so it shouldn't matter if it self-locked. I yanked on it even harder, kicked the door, screamed at it. Come on, dream door. Open. Up. Now. Erna? You in there? You mind removing yourself from Mitchell's lap long enough to answer the door, maybe?

The early-morning sun found the east-facing window. Light prismed all the hell over the place. My skin felt unreasonably hot, Hiroshima-afterblast hot, ready to melt at the slightest touch.

I threw a shoulder at the door, hoping the dream construction crews who dealt with 1972 used cheap flakeboard. But the door held firm.

I slammed my shoulder into it, then again, and again, throwing an increasing amount of body weight with every blow.

Still nothing.

The sun was blazing through the window at the end of the hall in earnest now. I raised my left hand to shield my eyes and immediately felt a searing pain, like I'd grabbed the wrong end of a hot curling iron. I glanced up through watery eyes just in time to watch a beam of light burn away two of my fingers.

First the ring finger.

Then the pinky.

A scream forced its way out of my mouth, and then I jerked my hand away from the light. Pressed my back up against the door. Did a beam of sunlight really just slice through my fingers like it was a light saber?

I forced myself to look down. My ring and pinky fingers were on the floor, at my feet.

They weren't severed. Not in the traditional sense, anyway. There was no blood, no ripped flesh or exposed bone. They were Play-Doh fingers, detached from a Play-Doh hand.

After a few seconds they begin to fade away and disappear completely.

III

THE THING WITH THREE FINGERS

I WOKE UP ON A hospital gurney with a skull-crushing headache and a raw throat. People in blue smocks brushed against my bed, which was jammed up against a wall in a busy hallway. Every time the bed jolted it sent another sledgehammer tap on the spike slowly inching its way to the center of my brain. My mouth tasted like dirty pennies. I wanted to throw up.

After a while I rolled over and used the metal rails to pull myself up to a sitting position. I ran my fingertips across my five-day stubble, patted my chest, my belly. All there. I was still wearing my nylon shorts and T-shirt. The ring and pinky fingers were still attached to my left hand.

But both were dead numb, like I'd fallen asleep on them. They wouldn't bend either. Not unless I cheated and used my other hand, which I noticed was now hooked up with an IV needle. Good Christ, what had happened last night?

Somebody blew past my gurney, flipping through papers on a clipboard.

"Hey," I called out, and the guy stopped midstride.

"Yeah?"

"Where am I?"

"Frankford Hospital, man. You O.D.'d."

"I *what*? How did I get here?"

"Girlfriend brought you in. She was pretty freaked out. I were you, I'd think about help. But I can't be the first person to tell you that."

And then he continued on down the hall.

O.D.'d?

I needed to get out of here. I grabbed the IV needle with the three good fingers of my left hand, yanked it out, sat up. Some blood shot out, so I pulled up the tape and recovered the puncture. I hated needles.

So this was Frankford Hospital. I hadn't been inside this place in years—and that had been the old building, which had been razed and replaced by this one.

My grandpop was here somewhere, on one of these floors. For a moment I thought about stopping up to see him, just to get the obligation out of the way. I could kill two birds with one stone—recover from overdose, check; visit grandfather, check. But then I remembered I was shoeless, hungover and confused. I needed a shower and a nap. A nap to last at least a week.

And I needed to make sure Meghan was okay, and that she didn't think I was a complete dick.

Once I was reasonably sure I wasn't going to puke, I swung my legs over the side of the gurney then slid off. My first few steps were wobbly, but okay. I walked out of the hospital. Nobody tried to stop me. And why would they? I was just a junkie in nylon shorts and a threadbare T-shirt. Hell, I was doing them a favor.

I made the four-block walk back to the apartment, carefully avoiding beads of glass on the sidewalk. One old woman, wrapped in a dirty gray shawl and a badly stained and ripped dress, stared at me from the doorway of a long-closed delicatessen. There was shock and anger in her eyes.

"It's you! You finally showing your face around here?"

Welcome home, Mickey Wade.

"You son of a bitch!"

I kept walking.

MEGHAN HAD LOCKED THE door. But she'd also thought to put the key under the doormat, bless her soul. I could only imagine what I'd put her through last night. No wonder she hadn't stuck around.

Inside the apartment the sofa bed was still pulled out, covers mussed, pillows twisted up and askew. Boxes had been pushed out of the way. I must have blacked out in bed. She panicked, called 911.

I pressed my face against the pillow that had been hers. It smelled like her—vanilla and the sweetest slice of fruit you can imagine. So at least that part hadn't been a dream. Meghan had really been here last night.

And somehow I'd managed to O.D. on beer and Tylenol.

There was nothing in Grandpop Henry's microscopic fridge except two Yuenglings from the night before. I didn't feel like walking back downstairs to buy something sensible for breakfast, like a Diet Coke or bottle of Yoo-Hoo. So I twisted open a beer. Maybe a beer would outsmart my headache. And if the headache wasn't fooled, the cold would at least soothe my throat. Besides, isn't this what unemployed writers are supposed to do? Drink a cold beer at eight in the morning?

I opened my laptop to search the job boards. There wasn't much to search—not for unemployed journalists, anyway. In years past, an out-of-work journalist could fall back on teaching or public relations. But now actual teachers and public relations flacks were duking it out, death match–style, for the same jobs. Journos didn't stand a chance.

My eyelids felt like slabs of concrete, so I gave up, drank a few more sips of beer and then crashed on the couch—bed. Somewhere in the haze of unconsciousness I heard my cell ring once. I reached up with my left hand, fingers still numb, fumbling for the phone, half-hoping it was Meghan. Nope; my mom. I hit the ignore button and closed my eyes. She probably wanted to know if I'd found a job yet. Or visited my grandpop yet. Or stopped being a screw-up yet.

SOMETIME LATER, THE RUMBLE of the El woke me up.

I was more than a little alarmed to discover that the two fingers on my left hand were *still* numb. Why hadn't the feeling come back yet? Maybe I whacked them on something on my way to the hospital, causing some nerve damage. Which would be fantastic. What did an unemployed writer need with fingers, anyway?

I rolled off the couch, starving. But Grandpop's cupboards were stocked with nothing but old-man junk food—a couple of cans of tuna, cream of tomato soup, a box of stale crackers and a foil bag containing some potato chip particulates. Maybe I could stick my face into the bag, inhale some nutritional value.

I settled on the tuna, but it took me awhile to find a can opener. I finished one can and then ate every single stale flakeboard cracker, washing them down with tap water, which tasted like salt and metal.

Okay, enough stalling. I grabbed my cell from the top of the houndstooth couch. It was time to call Meghan and start my awkward apology. And maybe find out what the hell had happened.

First I listened to my mom's message:

"Mickey, it's your mom. Just checking in to see how you're making out over there. Have you stopped by the hospital to see your grandfather yet?"

Yes, Mom, I could truthfully tell her, *I visited the hospital first thing this morning.*

"Anyway, maybe you could come up to have dinner with Walter and me this weekend. He's been asking about you. Let me know and I'll pick you up."

Walter is her boyfriend. I couldn't stand him. She knows this, but pretends not to know this. I hit erase.

The cell was down to a single bar, so I looked for a place to charge it. I found a black power cord that snaked across the floor, around a cardboard box and into the back of something hidden under a stack of file folders. To my surprise, it turned out to be a silver Technics turntable.

The thing looked thirty years old. I hit the power button on the silver tuner beneath it, then ran my index finger under the needle and heard a scratching, popping sound. It worked.

I fished out one of my father's albums—Sweet's *Desolation Boulevard*—and listened to "The Six Teens" while I finished off the warm Yuengling I'd opened a few hours ago.

This was the first time I'd listened to any of these albums.

The LPs were my dad's. Mom gave them to me on my twenty-first birthday. She told me I used to love to look at them when I was a toddler. Now, I haven't owned a record player since I was eight years old—a Spider-Man set, with detachable webbed speakers. So all these years I've had no way of listening to these albums. But now and again I'd open the three boxes full of old LPs and thumb through them, taking the time to soak up the art.

You can have your tiny little CD covers, or worse, your microscopic iPod jpegs. Give me LP covers, like George Hardie's stark black-and-white image of a blimp bursting into flames from *Led Zeppelin I*. Or the floating tubes on the front of Mike Oldfield's *Tubular Bells*. The freaky black-and-white lion's head on the cover of *Santana*, which I'd often misread as having something to do with *satan*. The Stones turning into cockroaches on *Metamorphosis*.

Grand Funk Railroad, Iron Butterfly, The Stones, Lou Reed, Styx—these were all bands that I loved purely for their cover art.

As for the music inside . . . well, my mileage varied. You could only listen to "In-a-Gadda-Da-Vida" so many times, if you know what I mean.

But I would look at the art and think about my dad bringing the albums home from the record shop—probably Pat's on Frankford Avenue—putting his headphones on, listening to the music, staring at the covers himself, letting his imagination wander, dreaming of making his own records someday.

But he never did make a record. He was killed before he had the chance.

WHILE MY CELL CHARGED I showered, pulled on a T-shirt and jeans, then ventured out for some food. First, I needed money. There was a battered ATM near the Sav-N-Bag market all the way down Frankford Avenue, near the end of the El tracks. The walk was as depressing as I imagined it would be. Shuttered storefronts. Abandoned shells of fast-food chains that became clinics for a while before they shut, too.

At the ATM I quickly checked my surroundings for possible muggers, then quickly shoved in my card and pressed the appropriate keys. I asked for $60—just enough to buy some cold cuts, maybe a few cans of soup, some boxes of cereal. Bachelor staples.

My request is granted, but my receipt tells me I only have $47 to my name.

Whoa whoa whoa. That didn't make any sense. It should have been more like $675. Where was my final paycheck from the newspaper? Today was Friday. Payday. My last one. Possibly ever.

By some miracle I got the *City Press*'s assistant HR guy on my cell. Funny that the paper can afford to get rid of writers and art designers but never management. The paper currently had a three-man human resources department; with me gone, there was exactly one news reporter on staff. Exactly which humans would these HR people be resourcing?

The assistant HR guy—Howard—explained that my last check has been all but wiped out by sick days I owed the paper.

"No no. That can't be right."

Howard assured me it was.

"I never took sick days. I was a reporter—I was out of the office a lot. You know, doing reporting."

Howard told me his hands were tied.

"Look, Howard, seriously, you're wrong about this. Check with Foster."

Howard asked who Foster was.

"Star Foster. The editor in chief? You know, of the paper?"

Howard told me it wouldn't matter if he spoke with Foster, or what she might say. He had my time sheets in front of him. He goes by the time sheets.

"You don't understand. I want . . . no, I *need* my entire final pay-check."

Howard told me he was sorry, wished me all the best, then hung up.

Which meant that unless I changed Howard's mind, I had exactly $47—plus the $60 I just withdrew—to last me pretty much forever.

Like most of America, I had nothing saved. Every month I danced so close to zero, my checking account was more like a temporary way station for a small amount of cash that passed between a newspaper and a series of credit card companies, corporations and utilities.

My economic strategy thus far had been simple: if I start to run out of cash, I slow down on spending until the next payday. That strategy, of course, depended on there *being* a next payday.

Mom was not an option. Not yet, anyway. Placing me in Grandpop's apartment was her brand of help—a gentle suggestion, not a handout. Asking for a loan now would just confirm my mother's lifelong theory that the Wadcheck men could never hang on to anything: marriage, fatherhood (my grandfather), songs, recordings, his life (my father), a relationship, a career (me). I was on my own.

I had written hundreds of articles and interviewed everyone in the city, from the power brokers to crooked cops to addicts squatting in condemned warehouses. And for three years, thousands of people had read my work and knew my byline. The name on my debit card was even starting to get recognized in bars and restaurants. *Are you the Mickey Wade who writes for the* Press?

Nope. I'm just some idiot standing outside a supermarket in my old neighborhood with no job and about sixty bucks in my pocket.

"You bastard."

I turned, and it was the old lady from this morning, leaning against the stone wall of the supermarket. She looked even rattier up close. Bad teeth, rheumy eyes. She must hang out on Frankford Avenue all day, waiting for losers to cross her path so she can mock them. She pointed at me with a crooked, bony finger.

"The day's going to come when you're going to get what's coming to you."

Oh, how I've missed Frankford.

A COPY EDITOR AT the *Press* named Alex Alonso once told me about the three basic things humans needed to survive. He'd worked one of those Alaskan fishing boat tours where you endure an exhaust-

ing, nausea-filled hell at sea for two months in exchange for a nice payday at the end. Alex said it was pretty much eighteen hours of frenzied labor, followed by six hours of insomnia. And for two months he consumed nothing but apples, peanut butter, cheap beer and cocaine.

I've kept this handy factoid in my back pocket for years, ready to deploy if times got super-lean. Cocaine isn't cheap, but it also isn't essential. What kept Alex alive, he said, were the fiber (apples), protein (peanuts) and grains (in the beer, of course).

I was ready to go shopping.

The Sav-N-Bag hadn't changed a bit in twenty-five years—same dirty orange and yellow color scheme, same crowded aisles, same carts with one wheel that either refuses to spin or forces you to veer to the left your entire shopping trip. Same lousy food.

This was a low-rent neighborhood market that relied on customers without cars. Anybody with a car went to the decent supermarkets in Mayfair or Port Richmond.

Fortunately the Sav-N-Bag was running a special on a big plastic tub of peanut butter. Not a name brand, like Skippy or Jif or Peter Pan. Just generic peanut butter. I put it in my dirty plastic carry-basket, then added a bag of undersized apples. The tab came to nine dollars. Hell, on this budget, I was good for another month and a half.

My grocery order safely tucked inside a planet-strangling plastic bag, I walked back up Frankford Avenue and stopped at Willie Shahid's beer bodega on the ground floor of the apartment to buy the cheapest six-pack I could find: Golden Anniversary, for $4.99.

Willie—not that I knew his name yet—looked at me, probably thinking, *Wow, you've lost your girl and your taste in beer, all in one day. Welcome to Frankford.*

I ate dinner as the sun went down over the tops of the rowhomes of Frankford—four tablespoons of peanut butter, one apple and two cans of Golden Anniversary. When dinner was over, I still felt hungry. And not nearly drunk enough.

I tried Meghan, got her voice mail. I left a message:

"Hey, it's me. Mickey. Or, if you prefer, Mr. Wadcheck. Look, I'm really sorry about last night, and to be perfectly honest, I'm a little confused. If you don't totally hate my guts, please call me back, okay? Okay."

Okay.

I put another one of my dad's old albums on the turntable: Pilot's eponymous debut LP. I'd loved the second track, "Magic," when I was a kid, and wanted to hear it again as nature intended— with scratches and pops. The way my dad heard it.

The wah-wah guitars made my head hurt, though. I went into the bathroom and helped myself to two Tylenols. I wanted to take it easy, after all. You know us O.D.-ing, over-the-counter-pain-reliever junkies.

AND THEN IT HAPPENED again.

ONE MINUTE I WAS sitting up. The next, I was on the floor of the same strange office. There was the same brown paper taped up over the windows. Same potted fern. Same filing cabinets. Same lounge chair. Same desk. Same pudgy doctor sitting behind it.

The office was dead silent and stifling from the dry radiator heat. I could smell the burning dust.

What was going on? I had no idea. This all felt and looked real. This was not a daydream nor a fantasy. I was not hallucinating. Every sense I had told me the same thing: I was actually in this room.

Looking down, I saw that the ring and pinky fingers of my left hand were still missing. There was no wound, no scars. Just smoothed-over skin where the digits should be.

If this *was* a dream, then I was again in the past. I wondered what year this was, and started searching for my laptop—realizing a second later that I was being an idiot.

Meanwhile, Dr. DeMeo spun in his creaky metal chair and flipped a switch. A typewriter hummed. He cracked his knuckles, and within a few seconds the room was full of the machine-gun clacking of the keys. When was the last time I heard that noise? High school?

"Don't mind me, Doc," I said. "Just going to help myself up off the floor here."

Dr. DeMeo continued typing, completely oblivious to me.

"You can't hear a word I'm saying, can you, you fat sweaty bastard?"

The typing stopped, but only because Dr. DeMeo had turned to look at something on his desk. Then he resumed his clack-clack-clack-clacking.

"Hey, you're a busy guy," I said. "It's okay with me."

I took a few steps forward and peeked over Dr. DeMeo's shoulder. As a writer, I considered such a thing an inexcusable sin, punishable by dismemberment. But DeMeo couldn't see me, so what did it matter?

```
Subject took 500 mg. fell into a restful sleep
within 2 min. Subject woke approximate 90 min-
utes later and proceeded to describe the test
room in great, yet vague detail. Pressing him
on questions such as what color was the carpet?
How many drinking glasses on the table? Did
```

you notice anything of note on the walls? resulted in generalities meant to coax clues
from investigator. It is the investigator's be-
lief that patient was trying to fake a success-
cessful experience by supplying details vague
enough to appear

He stopped typing and leaned back in his chair, almost smacking into me.

"Erna?" he asked. "Is that you?"

Not by a long shot, big boy.

DeMeo heaved himself forward to check his handwritten notes
again. I glanced at the date on the top of the report:

February 25, 1972

So okay, I was still stuck in this dream about the past. A past I
could see, smell, touch and hear. I was pretty sure I'd be able to
taste something if I licked it. Like, say, the half-eaten doughnut on
DeMeo's desk. But I wasn't ready for that kind of experimentation
yet. I didn't know where DeMeo's mouth had been.

The doctor spun himself back to his typewriter. The machine-
gun clacking resumed.

I slipped out the front door as quickly and quietly as possible. Did
he notice the door as it opened for a quick second, then slammed
shut on its own? I had no idea and honestly didn't give a shit.

DOWNSTAIRS, FRANKFORD AVENUE WAS quiet. There weren't many
cars, just a few people strolling up and down the sidewalks. The
stores were long closed, but a few bars and delis were doing some

business with drunks and late-night workers. It was cold. I walked to the corner and stared down Margaret Street.

One thing I haven't mentioned yet: I grew up around the corner from my grandpop's apartment.

Literally.

Darrah Street runs parallel to Frankford Avenue, one block away. The street was named for a Revolutionary War heroine named Lydia Darragh. According to legend, she overheard British plans to ambush Washington's army. She told friends she had to buy some flour from a mill in Frankford. Along the way, she snitched to the Americans, then bought her flour and went home. As a result of her trip to Frankford, the attack was a bust and dozens of American lives were spared—including, possibly, George Washington's. No idea why the city leaders dropped the "g" from Darragh's last name when it came time to honor her with a street (formerly a path located near the flour mill). No idea if the story is even true. But it came in handy for a history report or two in grade school.

Other than that, Darrah Street didn't have much going for it. In 2002, my mom finally moved to Northwood, which was considered the "upscale" part of Frankford.

A few years later, not long after I'd joined the *City Press* as a staff writer, I came across a press release from the state attorney general's office detailing the bust of a citywide heroin ring. One of the addresses jumped right out at me: the 4700 block of Darrah Street. I couldn't believe it. A heroin ring, right on the block where I grew up! I called the state attorney general's press flack for more details, thinking there might be a column in it. As it turned out, it wasn't just my old block. The drug ring operated out of *my childhood home*.

I checked the names of the accused, then called my mom.

She confirmed it: she'd unknowingly sold her home to a pair of (alleged) heroin dealers.

"They seemed like a nice young couple."

I'm sure they did. Who knew they'd head up an organization that would (allegedly) sell hundreds of thousands of dollars worth of big H all over the city?

Still, it was unsettling to learn that the house you grew up in, took your first steps in, read your first books in, wrote your first stories in, felt up your first girlfriend in would be the future HQ of people who spent their days stuffing horse into tiny plastic baggies.

I never pursued the story.

IF TODAY WAS REALLY February 25, 1972, then I was three days old and asleep in my crib, just one block away.

I wondered how far I could push this dream.

This stretch of Darrah Street was half residential, half industrial—small rowhomes on one side, a fire station and factory on the other. Everybody who lived on the rowhome side would look out their front windows and constantly be reminded of work. Everybody who worked across the street was constantly reminded of home.

I stood on the opposite side of the street, staring at my childhood home. What seemed so big to me as a kid now looked absurdly cramped through adult eyes. My parents' black Dodge Dart was parked out front. The porch hadn't been painted white yet; I remember my dad doing that when I was five or six years old, and me "helping" him. Now it was all the original brown brick and tan cement. There was a light on in the living room window.

From across the street I could hear myself crying.

At least I assumed it was me. The wailing seemed to come from directly behind the front window of 4738. And I was the only baby in the house at the time.

I looked both ways—the street was dead—then crossed and walked up the three concrete steps to my old front porch. It felt like walking onto the set of a children's school play. Everything was so tiny.

I'd also forgotten what the interior of our home looked like growing up. It was straight out of the pages of *Urban Hippie Digest*: red velvet walls, brown rugs. A Buddha statue had been placed in the corner, surrounded by incense holders and ashtrays. A console TV—a hand-me-down, chipped in places. My mom was sitting on a hand-me-down couch. I remembered climbing on that couch until the frame threatened to break under my weight.

My mom was shaking. No—*sobbing*. Face in her hands.

There was a baby bassinet across the room. It shook a little, too. I couldn't see myself, but I heard my unrelenting cries. I was either hungry, or I'd befouled myself. Didn't matter. I needed some sort of attention.

Come on, Mom. What are you waiting for? Pick me up! Where's my dad? Why won't he pick me up?

Then I remembered. I'd been born on a Tuesday; this would be Friday. Gig night. My dad and his band would be out on a job.

My crying just wouldn't stop. I felt my hands tremble. Why won't she pick me up? Was she already tired of me?

Before I knew what I was doing, my right hand was up. I made a fist and started pounding on the window.

IV

MY FATHER'S KILLER

Y MOTHER LOOKED UP. Her face was bright red. God, she was young. So, so young.

"Someone there?" she asked, her voice muffled by the glass.

I panicked and darted to the left of the window.

"Hello? *Is someone there?*"

After a few seconds I saw her face appear in the window, nervously peering outside from behind the parted curtains. I stopped breathing for a moment. She was only eighteen years old when I was born, but that age is an abstract concept. She's always been my mother, always been eighteen years older than me. Except now. Now I was a ghost standing on the porch of my childhood home, I was thirty-seven years old, and I was looking at the face of the woman who gave birth to me—suddenly two decades younger. And she's been crying. Her cheeks were still damp with tears, her eyes tender and red. She looked lost. Alone. Scared. Freaked out. Everything.

And her husband was out in a bar somewhere in Frankford—or maybe nearby Kensington. She probably told him she'd be fine handling the baby alone, but what choice did she have? They needed the money. They had a new mouth to feed.

After a while she moved away from the window and started talking to the baby, me, in a robotic monotone. *Okay,* she said. *Okay, I'm coming. Stop crying, I'm coming. Stop crying.*

I STARTED FEELING LIGHT-HEADED and dizzy again. I didn't know if I'd wake up in the same place where I'd fallen asleep, but I didn't want to chance waking up on Darrah Street in the middle of the night.

On the way back upstairs I ran into the red-haired kid again. He was sitting near the top of the first staircase, knees spread and hands curled into tight little fists. His green eyes, full of fury, bored right into mine. I wondered what I'd done wrong.

"You can still see me, huh?" I asked.

"Why do you keep asking me that? Of course I can see you. You're there, aren't you?"

"Where's your mom?"

He paused, looked down at his feet, then said:

"Out."

"You should tell your mom to stay home with you tonight instead of drinking in bars."

"Yeah? *You* tell her."

Then he stood, raced up the few steps to the second floor and slammed his door shut behind him. The noise echoed in the stairwell like a gunshot.

I waited a few moments, then made my way up to the third floor as silently as possible. I jiggled the knob on the door to 3-A. Still locked. I guess DeMeo had gone home for the night.

And then the door opened suddenly. The knob slipped out of my hand. DeMeo popped out from the doorway holding a small silver gun, which looked like a toy in his meaty fist.

He still couldn't see me—thank God. The barrel of the gun swung past my face a couple of times as he squinted out into the darkened hallway.

"Who's there?"

I took a few slow steps backward.

"I heard you rattling the knob! I know you're out there!"

I pressed my back against the opposite wall.

"There are no drugs here. No money. No nothing! Come back again and I'll blow your brains out."

I tried not to breathe. I prayed I suddenly didn't turn visible.

"Goddamn hippie junkies."

DeMeo gave the hallway a final up and down before ducking back inside.

I slid down until I was sitting on the hallway floor.

I don't know how long I stayed there, staring at nothing in the dark. At some point I heard the downstairs door open with a loud bang, high heels clicking on the tile floor of the foyer, a female voice muttering to herself. Cursing. There was the jangle of keys. I had a good idea I knew who it was.

"Go home to your kid," I said, then repeated it a little louder. *"Go home to your kid."*

I wished I could go to Brady's right now, confront my father, tell him:

Go home to your kid.

THE NAME ANTHONY WADE probably means nothing to you. But for a brief moment there, it could have.

The way my grandmom Ellie tells it, there was an exciting couple of weeks in early 1971 when my father's band, which was called Flick, was up in New York for a recording session that was

supposed to lead to a recording deal with one of the major labels. They kind of sounded like Chicago—the early Chicago. The *good* Chicago. Tight rhythm section, a powerful brass thing going on. Only they were from Philadelphia.

But it all went sour when an exec noticed the name of the band painted on the bass drum: FLICK.

Put the "L" and the "I" close together, it sort of looks like a "U."

The record exec noticed it midsession, and said there was no way he was gonna sign a band who put *that word* on the front of their drum set. My dad refused to change it. That was the name of the band, man.

Thing was, my dad knew that FLICK looked like *that word*. That was why he'd picked it, my grandmom had said.

"Your father always had a self-defeating sense of humor."

I was half-surprised he didn't go with CLINT.

A year after the New York thing went south, I was born. My dad worked an endless series of menial jobs to make ends meet, but he always played gigs on weekends—even when the band fell apart.

The horns went first; they were too much in demand, and found better-paying gigs easily. My father responded by buying something called a Guitorgan, which fills in chunky organ sounds by pressing your fingers on the frets (while still strumming the strings). This pissed off the keyboard player, who split and took the bass player with him around 1976. This didn't discourage my father. He simply added bass pedals he could play with his feet. By 1978 the drummer didn't see the point, so he left, too, only to be replaced by an electronic drum machine.

By then he was known as ANTHONY WADE, HUMAN JUKEBOX, and he'd take out little ads in the local papers. He played a bunch of local places.

Brady's was a small restaurant and bar right near the end of the

Market-Frankford El line. If you got drunk and hopped on an east-bound El train at City Hall, this is where you would be spit out. Just beyond Bridge and Pratt were a series of cemeteries. It was the end of the line on so many levels.

My parents took me to Brady's once, an hour before one of my dad's gigs. I felt like King Shit, sitting there, ordering up a cheese-burger and a Coke in a thick plastic mug loaded with ice, watch-ing my dad set up his equipment. This was my dad as Human Jukebox, so there was a lot of it. I remember feeling proud, watch-ing him up there. Pretty soon he'd be the center of attention. *My dad.*

The next time I saw Brady's I was a high school senior. I'd cut afternoon classes and went for a walk, ending up at Bridge and Pratt. The windows were dark; the door chained shut. It had closed not long after my dad had died.

YOU DON'T FORGET THINGS like the morning your mom tells you your dad's been killed.

God, the way she just said it.

Your father's been killed.

I asked her what had happened—had he been hit by a car? As a kid, the only way I could wrap my mind around death was to imag-ine a speeding car. I had been forbidden to cross Darrah Street and told that if I disobeyed, I could be hit by a car, and then I would die, and there would be no more Mickey.

But Mom told me no, your father got into a fight—*you know how much fighting gets you in trouble*—and the guy daddy was fighting hit him too hard and . . .

And what? I asked, all the while picturing the scene in my

mind, my father out on the hard sidewalks of Frankford, fists in the air, blocking punches and throwing some jabs of his own, just like Rocky Balboa.

And he died, she'd said.

Later, I'd ask her again about my father's death, and she'd tell me the same thing. He'd gotten into a stupid fight, and the guy hit back too hard, and that was that.

Whatever happened to the guy? I'd asked my mom.

Nothing.

Which didn't make sense to me. How could nothing have happened to a guy who'd killed somebody, accident or not?

As I got older, I filled in the gaps myself, inserting pieces of narrative my mom had left out. I imagined some drunk heckling my father. I imagined my dad angry, just like he got sometimes with me when I bothered him. I imagined him pushing some drunk guy in the bar, and the guy pushing back. Imagined my dad taking a swing and losing his balance and his head connecting with the sharp edge of the bar. Imagined the drunk guy saying it was an accident, and being allowed to go free.

In my mind, this version of my father's death quickly cemented itself into fact. This was the version I told friends when they learned that my father was dead. This was the version I embellished for an essay I wrote freshman year of college for Advanced Composition 2. That essay ("My Father's Killer") ended up being reprinted in the campus English Department quarterly and had the side effect of launching my journalism career when a professor named Jack Seydow encouraged me to write for the campus paper.

And according to that version of the story, the guy who killed my father was just some drunk son of a bitch who threw one punch too hard.

"My Father's Killer," I'd hinted at in my essay, was himself. He'd done it to himself. And I had a hard time forgiving him for that.

Pretty much my whole life.

MY HEAD FELT THICK, full of sand. I pressed my palms against my eyes and saw stars and comets and nebulae racing toward me. I wondered how long I'd be here, sitting in this dark hallway in February 1972 before the dream ended. Would the sun come up again and blast-burn another part of me away? My arms? My head? Maybe the sun would finish me off this time?

And then I woke up.

MEGHAN WAS STARING AT me. Her blond hair was damp and smelled like shampoo. The cleanest, most intoxicating shampoo in the world. She was crouched down on one knee and was touching my chest.

"Mickey?"

I blinked a few times, then patted the floorboards just to make sure they were real.

"Yeah. Hi. Uh, how did you get in here?"

"You left the door unlocked. I thought you said this was a bad neighborhood."

"Most muggers are too lazy to walk up to the third floor."

She sat down, crossed her legs, then reached out to touch my forehead. I must have been a sight. She takes me first thing in the morning to the emergency room of a hospital. Now she finds me passed out on the floor.

"How are you," she said.

"I'm okay."

The look on her face told me she didn't believe me. I didn't believe me either.

"You want anything? I brought some turkey sandwiches. Some Vitamin Water."

"No, really I'm fine."

She noticed the turntable, and the *Pilot* LP. I heard the needle running over and over and over in the final groove.

"Pilot . . . wow. I think my dad had that album. You been taking a spin back to yesteryear?"

I bit my tongue like you wouldn't believe.

We stayed there on the floor for a while. I was seriously dizzy—like drunken bed spins without the drinking. The tiny elastic hoses that pump blood through my brain were writhing, throbbing. My mouth tasted like metal, and I could feel the thin layer of sweat beneath my clothes. It wasn't as bad as this morning, when I woke up in the hospital and it felt like my skull had been cracked open. But I also didn't want to go moving around too much. Not yet.

I checked the fingers on my right hand. Still attached. Still numb.

Then I finally pushed myself to a sitting position, across from Meghan.

"I'm sorry about what happened last night," I said. "I didn't meant to scare you like that."

"So what happened?"

"I was kind of hoping you could tell me."

"You don't remember?"

I remembered a lot of things, but I wasn't exactly sure they were real. The last thing I wanted was to make this conversation even more awkward. So I lied.

"Last thing I remember," I said, "I was in bed with you. Wait . . . that sounds wrong. I was on the *couch* with you. I nodded off, and what was it. What did I miss?"

Meghan looked at me.

"You were mumbling in your sleep. Saying something like, you can't hear me, you can't see me. Then you said something about all of this being a dream."

"How did I get to the hospital?"

"A little before seven you started convulsing, which really freaked me out. I tried waking you up. You wouldn't. Then you started screaming with your eyes shut, so I called 911. They asked me if you were on any drugs, but I told them I didn't know."

As she spoke, I replayed last night's dream in my head. While Meghan had been watching me convulse, I'd probably been throwing my shoulder against an imaginary door, trying to break it down. I screamed when my imaginary fingers fell off.

Meghan took me by the shoulders now. Stared hard into my eyes.

"Mickey, I know you're between jobs and everything, but if you need to see somebody, I can help you out."

"I don't need help. I'm just a little tired."

"Nobody drinks a six-pack then lapses into a near-coma, Mickey. It just doesn't make sense. You always seem broke . . ."

"Wait, wait—you think I'm on drugs?"

"I'm not accusing you of anything. I'm not here to judge. Jesus, I sound like a therapist . . . look, I dated a guy in college with a serious problem, and we all got him some help. It took awhile, but he's doing okay now."

"Meghan, I swear to you, it's not drugs. I'm too broke to afford drugs. I had those Yuengling and a couple of aspirin. That was it. You were here with me the whole time, remember?"

"Aspirin, huh?"

"From my grandfather's medicine cabinet. Unless you think he was doing drugs and stashing them in the Tylenol bottle."

Meghan touched my face as if she could read minds with her fingertips. I was angry, but part of me softened at her touch.

"Okay, Mickey. Maybe you just need some rest."

"Yeah. Maybe."

She stood up and started looking through her purse for her keys. As much as I wanted her to stay, I also wanted time to sort through what I'd just dreamed about. All of it was so damn real, so detailed.

"Let me walk you."

"I'm fine—I'm parked right downstairs. You act like this is Beirut or something."

"Yeah, I know it's not Beirut. Beirut has more buildings left standing."

Meghan leaned down and brushed her lips against my forehead. I reached up and touched her arm, as if my touch could make her linger. But she pulled away quickly and walked to the door. She smiled, told me she'd check on me later.

I pushed myself up off the floor and went to the bathroom for more Tylenol. The two I'd taken before hadn't done a damn thing—

Wait a minute.

V

THE CLOCKWISE WITNESS

USING A BUTTER KNIFE, I chopped a single pill into quarters, doing the math in my head. Last night, I'd popped four pills, 250 milligrams each. I had weird-ass dreams about cars and women in polka-dot dresses and fat, sweaty doctors that lasted pretty much all night long.

This evening I'd taken two pills, and the weird-ass dream thing lasted three, maybe four hours.

So a quarter of a single pill would be what . . . a half hour?

Okay, worst case, I'd swallow it and it wouldn't do a thing. Then I'd know it was something else making me dream about February 1972. But if it had been the pills, it would start to explain a lot. Namely, that all of these crazy dreams weren't coming out of nowhere.

I opened a grape Vitamin Water that Meghan had brought and swallowed the quarter pill. Then I laid back down on the floor, next to the couch, and closed my eyes.

There was no warning, no herald. The pill worked that fast.

WITHIN SECONDS I WAS on the floor of the dark, empty office. Two fingers, still missing. El rumbling outside. This time, however, I stayed put in the office that would someday become my Grandpop's apartment. As Blaise Pascal once wrote: "All of man's trouble stems from his inability to sit quietly in a room alone."

Instead, I peeled back some of the cardboard, looked out of the front windows and watched the soft rain land on the early 1970s cars moving down Frankford Avenue. I listened to wet tires against asphalt, a soothing sound broken up every few minutes by the thunder of the arriving El that always, without fail, jolted me, whipping shadows across my face.

There were also murmured voices somewhere in the apartment building. A woman's. Then an angry kid, saying he didn't understand, he *was* being quiet. And then the woman's voice again, saying something about being done, that's it, she couldn't take it anymore. Ah, another quiet night in Frankford circa 1972.

Right? This *was* 1972?

But I didn't want to go outside and check. I just wanted to sit on that weird stiff psychiatrist's sofa and take everything in. Convince myself that I was actually sitting here in the past.

Everything felt real. I could smell the burning dust in the air, baked by the steam radiator in the corner. I could hear the rumble of the El outside. The squeal of the brakes. The thump of the doors opening, then closing. I could feel the fibers of the cushion beneath me, the smooth polished wood of the sofa's frame. I could blink and breathe. I was able to run my tongue around inside my mouth.

But this couldn't really be my physical body, could it? Meghan said she'd watched my body in the present—mumbling, convulsing and otherwise seeming to have a perfectly good time by itself.

So what part of me was sitting here right now? My soul? Spirit? Life force? Ghost? Whatever it was, this *other me* was able to walk downstairs and open doors and pick up newspapers. In fact, except for being invisible to most people and that pesky "dissolved by light" thing, this *other me* acted just like my physical body.

I thought that maybe I should stand up, test my limitations. Find something this body could do that my real body couldn't.

But it was too late; time was up. I felt the familiar dizziness wash over me, and then one violent head nod later . . .

I was back.

I SPENT THE WEEKEND experimenting—nights only. I quickly learned that whatever time of day I popped a pill, that would be the time of day I'd wake up back in the past. Early Saturday morning I took a quarter of a pill, all excited to continue my experimenting, but then almost baked myself alive in the bright, glare-filled office—despite the cardboard taped over the windows. I crawled under DeMeo's desk and curled myself up into a quivering little ball until the pill wore off.

So by day, I crashed. The pills left me exhausted and headachy, with my body temperature going up and down at random. It all felt vaguely like the flu. I listened to my father's albums to distract me from the pain.

The only part of my body that didn't ache were the two numb fingers on my left hand. I found some medical tape in the medicine cabinet and used them to make a crude splint. I can't tell you how many times I accidently bent them backwards on the cherrywood desk or the couch because I forgot they were there.

From time to time my cell rang, and I would reach up and turn its face toward me and see that is was Mom calling again. Didn't she get the hint by now that I pretty much never picked up the phone, that I always let her calls go to voice mail? She was unstoppable, though, leaving messages about visiting Grandpop, my job hunt, or coming to dinner—three things I had no intention of pursuing anytime in the near future.

My mom didn't realize that pushing me resulted in an equal and opposite reaction. Or maybe she did realize, and hoped that at some point I'd snap and the physics would reverse, like the North and South Poles after a massive demagnetization.

So I ignored her.

Meghan called twice, but I couldn't bring myself to listen to her messages. There was still a good chance I was caught on a downward spiral of insanity, and I wanted to avoid sucking her down with me. This, after all, was my pill-popping lost weekend. Just me, the pills, some peanut butter, sixes of Golden Anniversary beer and a bunch of LPs that used to belong to a dead hippie musician. You don't bring people you care about along for a ride like that.

Besides, what did I think—that we had a future together? I was a philanthropic gesture. A novelty. Sooner or later Meghan moved on to something else. I'd watched it happen. No, I had to go this alone.

So by day I ate peanut butter and apples. If it was late enough in the afternoon, I had a few cold Golden Anniversaries. They actually weren't bad if you drank them fast enough.

And by night I jumped around the early 1970s.

THE MORE I PRACTICED, the better my aim. The human mind is capable of all kinds of amazing tricks. Like telling yourself the night before that you want to wake up at a certain time in the morning. More often than not, you'll wake up at that time—even beating the alarm clock you set as a backup.

So whenever I popped a pill, or the sliver of a pill, I started thinking hard about the date I wanted.

February 24.

February 28.

March 10.

March 30.

And so on.

No matter how hard I tried, I couldn't go back beyond the day I was born—February 22, 1972. This seemed to be the default line, and it was disappointing. The journalist in me had fantasies about going back to November 22, 1963, staking out the grassy knoll in Dallas and putting that nearly fifty-year-old story to bed. *Dear Oliver Stone,* my e-mail would begin . . .

But nothing doing. If I concentrated on February 21, 1972—or any day preceding it—I ended up back in February 22, 1972, by default.

I also couldn't go back to a time I'd already visited. Maybe this was a built-in protection feature to prevent me from ripping open the fabric of reality, or something.

It worked.

NOR COULD I VENTURE much beyond 1972. Saturday night I decided I wanted to see the Bicentennial, and my dad playing with his band near Penn's Landing. This was one of my earliest memories: being down near the riverfront; seeing the tall ships; the red, white and blue streamers; and my father, Anthony Wade, strumming his guitar outside of a restaurant—just one of dozens of musicians hired by the city that day. I'd gotten lost at one point, and wandered off to a restaurant boat nearby along with my aunt, who was only nine months older. Some cop had found us, luckily, and all was good. Sometimes I wonder what would have happened if he hadn't. If we'd stayed lost. It was probably this combination of fear and excitement that imprinted the day forever in my mind.

So I popped four pills and thought hard about the night of July 4, 1976. I concentrated on the date, repeated it to myself over and over and over. I imagined fireworks. Red, white and blue streamers everywhere. Penn's Landing. Liberty bells. The restaurant ship— the *Moshulu*. The bustle of the crowd. The sound of my father's band playing. Every possible detail I could squeeze out of my own head. Again I repeated the date out loud. I went all method—I *became* the date.

The moment I woke up in the office, however, I didn't feel right. I was dizzy and easily distracted. *Oooh, look at the pretty cars. The speeding El . . . oooh! A pigeon!* Somehow I made it down the stairs and out the front door to Frankford Avenue, which was alive and full of noise and kids screaming. Just make it to the El, I told myself. But the farthest I got was two steps on the sidewalk before I got dizzy, did a head nod and woke up back at home.

The pills wanted me to stick to a particular time frame.

THE PILLS ALSO WANTED me to stay in the dark. I realized that losing my fingers wasn't a fluke incident. Direct light of any kind—be it sun, a lamp or even a flashlight—did my time-traveling body serious harm. When I walked down Frankford Avenue and strayed too close to a neon sign, *I felt it.* I moved away, I felt better. If I lingered beneath a streetlamp, I would feel dizzy, and my ghostly eyes would water. It didn't take long to put it together that light equals harm. And in big enough doses, it meant the permanent kind of harm. It was best to stay in the shadows completely.

Again I wondered about this ghostlike "body" I used in the past. Was everyone's soul or spirit or ghost or whatever this sensitive to light? Is this the way we evolved flesh-and-blood bodies—to protect ourselves?

It's questions like these that keep you up at night, making you giddy and terrified at the same time.

SOMEWHERE IN THAT TIMELOST weekend it occurred to me that I could have the solution to all of my problems right here in this Tylenol bottle.

I was jobless and broke. Surely I could think of a way to use the pills to turn a small buck or two?

Nothing audacious, nothing that would screw with the thin, gossamer fabric of the space-time continuum. I've watched enough bad science fiction movies to know the rules. I also realized that if it were possible to travel back into the past to steal things, countless priceless artifacts would have gone missing on a regular basis. There would be no crown jewels. No *Mona Lisa*. No Hope Diamond. No moon rocks. Nothing cool at all. Future time-thieves would have nicked them all.

So after a while, I came up with the idea of vintage paperbacks and comic books.

Think about it. They were mass produced, cheap and wouldn't be missed in their own time. And they were worth a great deal more in the present.

When I'd been gainfully employed at the *City Press*, I would sometimes hop across town and waste a Saturday afternoon scouring the shelves of a mystery bookstore called Whodunit. Most of the stuff was affordable—five or seven bucks for a Gold Medal hardboiled paperback that originally cost a quarter. But there were some real rarities that went for $20, $30 or even $50. Of course, these tended to be elusive titles from my favorite hardboiled writers—David Goodis, Jim Thompson, James M. Cain, Fredric Brown, Dan J. Marlowe.

A quarter in one year, $50 in another. I was no Wharton School grad, but even I could see this was an amazing return on investment.

So I did a trial run to see if I could carry something back to the present. I took a half pill, went back to March 30, 1972. I walked across the street. On the rack was a fresh copy of *Marvel Spotlight #2: Werewolf by Night.*

I'd never owned the original. But parts of it, along with pages from later issues, had been cannibalized and turned into a book-and-record set, which my father left under the tree for me Christmas 1978. He loved the classic monsters—your Draculas, your Frankensteins, your Wolfmen. And I loved that book-and-record, even though it terrified the crap out of me.

Lingering by the comic rack, I finally reached for it, trying to play it all stealthy. I was invisible, so I had that going for me. No one could see me. Even if they could, who would think anything of a middle-aged guy standing near a newsstand? Still, I was nervous, like I was about to knock over a bank. My fingers fumbled. The slick cover slipped out of my grasp once, twice, three times. Could anyone see this? The world's lamest attempt at shoplifting ever?

After another eternity of hamfistedness, I regained my finger-hold on the thing and ran for it.

Over there, kids! Look at the invisible man with the stolen werewolf comic! Jogging across Frankford Avenue, avoiding the bright headlights, looking all nervous and guilty . . .

Back in the office I laid down on the floor and tightly pressed the comic to my chest with my palms. I closed my eyes and waited for the dizziness to wash over me.

. . .

I SNAPPED AWAKE AND immediately grasped at my chest with my eight good fingers.

No werewolf comic.

And with it, my idea of stealing comics and paperbacks from the past and eBaying them at a 400 percent markup in the future.

OTHER MONEYMAKING SCHEMES POPPED into my head, of course. I briefly thought about becoming a private eye. I could meet clients in the past, then use Google to "solve" their cases in the present. Only one problem, of course: almost nobody in the past could see me. Just that redheaded kid down on the second floor. What was I going to do, have a twelve-year-old kid be my Velda?

I could try to set up shop in the present, but there was a problem with that, too: unless I could find dozens of people who had burning questions about events from February 1972, I'd starve. There wasn't even a good Philadelphia tragedy I could witness firsthand and turn into a book. My time-traveling abilities were limited to the point of being useless.

The only thing the pills were good for, it seemed, was walking around Philadelphia during the first few months of my life and depressing the hell out of myself.

MY MOTHER GREW UP on the fringes of Frankford, near Bridge Street and Torresdale Avenue. The neighborhood is still alive, but you can tell it's had a few severe beatings. Along the way, the neighbors had gotten the idea that it was okay to throw their trash everywhere—the sidewalks, the gutter, their front porches.

Windows broke and stayed broken. A few blocks away, you could hear the constant rumble of I-95.

But you couldn't in late February 1972, because Interstate 95 hadn't been built yet.

There were no pimped-out SUVs with throbbing subwoofers cruising the tiny streets. There was no shuttered pizza shop or deli. There was very little trash in the street gutters. There were very few broken sidewalks and crumbled curbs. In 1972 this was just another quiet middle-class neighborhood in the middle of the night.

Standing across the street, I looked at the rowhome where my mom grew up, just four from the end of the block. All the lights were out except for one: the kitchen. Somewhere in that house my mom's father, Grandpop Ted, was probably enjoying his Saturday night, listening to polkas on the radio, drinking pull-top cans of Schaefer and burning through countless packs of Lucky Strikes. Grandpop Ted would die eighteen years later. Lung cancer.

So was I standing here for a reason? Was I supposed to cross Bridge Street, knock on the door and ask him to kindly cut back on the smoking?

After my dad was killed I spent a lot of nights in that house on Bridge Street, crashing on the green shag carpet in the living room. I'd listen to Grandpop Ted talk to Grandma Bea, both of them drinking and smoking, polkas on the radio in the background. They'd laugh. They'd fight. I'd curl up into a ball and cry a lot, but not so they could hear me.

Maybe I should walk back to my own house and leave a note for my mom:

HI ANNE!
LISTEN, THE GUITAR-PLAYING DUDE WITH A PONYTAIL YOU JUST MARRIED? UNDER NO CIRCUMSTANCES SHOULD YOU

LET HIM OUT OF THE HOUSE ON SUNDAY, DECEMBER 7, 1980.
TRUST ME ON THIS.

SIGNED,
A FRIEND

I drifted back into Frankford proper, which was littered with the landmarks of my childhood. Instead of a grungy Sav-N-Bag there was a clean, shiny Penn Fruit Supermarket, with new carts and freshly painted walls and rows of boxes and cans and fruit and meat and bread. Farther down on Frankford Avenue there was a poultry shop, where rotisserie chickens would spin in a case near the front window. It was night, so the birds were gone, but the rotisserie machine was still there, along with a sign advertising whole chickens, halves, legs, breasts, thighs. My stomach rumbled at the sight. There was a Kresge's five-and-dime, with a luncheonette counter. There was a drugstore, not a chain, an honest-to-God neighborhood drugstore, also with a luncheonette counter. You could see it just beyond the front doors, even in the dark. There was a huge toy store named Snyder's. There were record shops. Children's clothing stores, where you could buy your kids their Easter outfits. There was a place to buy lingerie. There was a candy store. No cigarettes, no bread, no milk, no lottery tickets, no porn mags, no motor oil—just rows of Bit-o-Honeys and Swedish fish and sugared gum drops and Day-Glo jelly fruit slices and ovals of chocolate behind a vast glass counter. You could walk in with fifteen cents and walk out with a small white paper bag full of penny candy. Candy that actually cost a penny each.

You trash a place in your mind for so long you forget that you used to actually love it.

· · ·

I COULD WANDER ALL night, but it wouldn't change the truth. I was still a dead broke guy a few credits shy a college degree, living in a bad neighborhood without a job during the worst recession since the Great Depression. So what if I could pop pills and wake up in a different year? No one could see me. No one could talk to me. I didn't matter to anyone now or in the present.

There *had* to be something I could do with these pills. But I wasn't smart enough to figure it out yet. Maybe my grandpop had it figured out.

Then I remembered the boxes and crates.

BACK IN THE APARTMENT I dove into the papers. What had I been thinking? He must have found a way to use the pills to his financial advantage. Clearly the man wasn't rich, but he got by. He had to have been up to something in this apartment all this time. And the clues were probably in these boxes and crates.

There were genealogy charts. Seemingly random newspaper clippings going back to the 1920s and running into the 1990s. Real estate listings. Birth notice pages. Medical reports. None of it organized. None of it made sense.

What was he doing?

For instance: one manila folder, marked "Crime Wave" in a shaky scrawl, was jammed with a series of clips from the local paper, the *Frankford Gleaner.* The articles detailed a series of break-ins and burglaries up and down Frankford Avenue during the summer of 1979. Totally friggin' random.

Unless my grandpop was taking the pills and much more adept

at pinpointing the year he visited? Was it possible he was going back to 1979 and looting the Avenue? And if so, how did he keep the stuff? Did he put everything into a bank safety-deposit box in the past, then open it in the present? Of course, that required the ability to open a box in the past, and you couldn't do that if you were invisible. And in a well-lit bank.

Maybe this was just a random series of articles he'd kept because he was a true-crime junkie. Maybe it meant nothing at all.

My head started to hurt.

After a few hours of searching I stumbled across a Florsheim shoe box. It was packed with old photos of my father. I cracked a Golden Anniversary and sat down to examine them.

I had never seen these before. A lot of them showed my father as a little boy, in short pants and everything. He was smiling and crouched next to Grandpop Henry, who—loathe as I am to admit this—*did* look a lot like me. He was wearing a V-neck T-shirt and smiling. He had more hair.

All of us Wadcheck men look alike. It was like the same guy was reborn again, and again, and again, with only minor genetic input from the mother.

And yes, there was Grandmom Ellie, beaming, holding my baby father in her arms. Presumably, Grandpop Henry had been the one taking the photo.

These photos offered glimpses of a world I barely knew existed—some magical fairy-tale kingdom where my dad was alive, and his parents were still married, they loved each other, and things still had the chance of turning out okay. The furniture was shabby, the walls were chipped, but they were just starting their lives together in a quiet Philadelphia neighborhood. They had no idea of the tragedies that awaited them.

The man in the V-neck T-shirt had no idea he'd be burying his son in about thirty years.

The woman holding the baby had no idea her husband would leave her, and she'd live more or less alone the rest of her life.

The baby had no idea that he would lose his temper in a bar and kick-start a thirty-second fight that would end his life.

I had another beer, then dug deeper into the box. I was surprised to see some grainy, orange-baked Polaroid photos of myself.

There was me, lounging with my dad on our threadbare brown living room rug. Me, hanging on to his arm, both of us sharing an oversized doughnut, the console TV in the background playing a *Star Trek* rerun. Me, pounding away on a toy organ, while Dad strummed his acoustic guitar. Me, hanging next to my father's band during his Bicentennial gig down at Penn's Landing. Which, if I indeed had stayed lost, would have probably been the last photo of me my parents would have seen.

What I *do* remember of the time I spent with my father was that it always revolved around music or horror movies or science fiction shows—in short, the things he liked to do. He was indoctrinating me. Giving me an early booster shot of the good stuff. Back then I was completely enthralled by him. I'd perch myself on the landing leading down to the basement, listening to my father running through chord changes or trying to pick up chords from Top 40 singles or organizing his records and lyric sheets in a filing cabinet. The basement air would always be thick with the aroma of cigarettes or pot.

Maybe, had he lived, we would have shared our first joint together.

OUTSIDE THE EL RUMBLED. I opened a Golden Anniversary and put on another of my father's albums—Styx's *Paradise Theatre*. This was one of the few in the collection that he'd never had a chance to hear. My father belonged to some album of the month club, and it arrived in the mail (along with Phil Seymour's *Phil Seymour*) a month after he died. My mom was too much of a wreck to notice I'd claimed the album for myself. And remember, this was two years before "Mr. Roboto" made it embarrassing to like Styx.

I finished my beer and wondered if maybe I really was losing my mind, and imagining all of this. Maybe *I* was the one lingering in a coma, victim of a drug problem I wasn't even aware I had.

At the bottom of a milk crate I found a scrapbook. It had big obnoxious brass rings holding the thick velvet cover and the stiff, crinkly pages together. It was the kind of photo album where you peel up the plastic, from left to right, place your photos on the white sticky backing, then smooth it back down. Unless you had the patience and steady hand of a sober monk, you'd always end up with crinkles. And it looked like Grandpop Henry had tied one on when he slapped this thing together.

I flipped through the pages for a few minutes before I realized I had been absolutely wrong about my father's death.

VI

THIS COULD BE THE LAST TIME

**Y FATHER, ANTHONY WADE,** the Human Jukebox, played three sets at Brady's, from nine until about eleven forty. That's when some witnesses say twenty-year-old William Allen Derace—because all killers come with three names—walked into Brady's, sat down, ordered a mug of Budweiser and a sirloin steak.

He sat in a booth alone, and watched my father, the Human Jukebox, perform some Stones, Doors and Elvis cover songs. Derace's steak remained untouched; it sat on top of wax paper in its red plastic basket until after the cops had come and gone. He did not drink any of his Bud.

And then at approximately 11:45, five minutes before my father was set to take a break, and in the middle of a guitar solo during his cover of the Rolling Stones' "The Last Time," Billy Allen Derace walked up to the stage, smiled, showed my father the steak knife in his hand, muttered something, then began to stab him in the chest.

By the second knife blow my father's aorta had been punctured, and he had probably gone into shock, but he still managed to lift his Guitorgan to parry the third strike. The *Daily News* had published a photo of the guitar, with a slash mark running down its black lacquered body and into the fret board. Derace stabbed

my father a fourth, a fifth, a sixth, then a final seventh time before a pair of off-duty firefighters pulled him away from the stage and subdued him. Derace, however, managed to wriggle free and escape through the back alley.

The whole thing took about thirty seconds.

BILLY DERACE WASN'T drunk. He hadn't consumed so much as a swallow of beer. The mug he'd ordered, which sat on the table, was untouched.

And my father's death wasn't a brawling "accident." Multiple witness interviewed by the Philadelphia Police Department, the *Philadelphia Bulletin* and the *Philadelphia Daily News* said that yeah, that crazy Billy Derace just strolled up to the tiny stage and started stabbing him in the chest with the steak knife. My dad didn't even have the chance to throw a punch. Moments later, Billy Derace was beaten to the ground.

Not long after, Billy Derace somehow vanished.

Police found Billy Derace at his then-current residence— nearby Adams Institute, which was (and is) one of the top psychiatric hospitals in the country. It has been around since 1813, first known as the Asylum for Persons Deprived of the Use of Their Reason, and later as Frankford Asylum for the Insane, and then finally the more PC-sounding Adams Institute, named after a wealthy family who had owned a buttload of farmland nearby and later lent their name to an adjacent avenue.

Two cops walked into the room with handcuffs and guns, but Billy Derace already had restraints around his wrists and ankles.

And he'd had them on for much of the past twenty-four hours, removed only for a sponge bath.

Derace, the doctors at the Adams Institute told police, was near comatose, with occasional fits and seizures. He was bound to the bed for his own protection.

One doctor was quoted: Mitchell DeMeo.

No, Dr. DeMeo said, my patient was definitely *not* anywhere near Brady's at Bridge and Pratt. Derace was here, in restraints, and checked hourly by the attending nurses. He'd been in a semi-vegetative state since 1979. Only recently had he shown signs of wakefulness. But to slip out of a mental hospital and make his way to a bar to stab a random guitar player? Impossible.

Mitchell DeMeo—the same man whose office would later become my grandpop's apartment.

To further his point, DeMeo even produced some time-stamped, black-and-white closed-circuit surveillance of the hospital grounds, which revealed Billy Derace did not leave the grounds at any point that week. Or at any point during the previous two years, for that matter.

The witnesses at Brady's, however, swore it was Derace. A few even knew him from around Frankford. Descriptions were given to a police sketch artist. The resulting sketch looked a hell of a lot like Billy Derace.

I was staring at a photocopy of the sketch now. My grandpop had somehow scored one, along with the full police report.

He also had clipped every single newspaper article about the murder, which honestly, wasn't much. A dead musician in a dive bar wasn't the stuff of front pages. The one-man-band thing gave it a strange little twist, but that was only good for a one-liner in the lead. Billy Derace was never definitively placed at the scene of the crime.

Who were you going to believe? A bunch of working-class folks half in their cups near midnight, or a team of the nation's top psychiatric doctors and nurses?

So Billy Derace was never convicted.

My mom had never spoken a word about this. Neither had my grandmother, or Grandpop for that matter.

But Grandpop obviously hadn't let it go.

AND HE HAD A bottle of pills in his medicine cabinet that would send him back to the past.

Why?

GRANDPOP USUALLY SEEMED ANNOYED by the rest of the family. He'd show up at holiday events, perch himself in a corner, then crack a lukewarm can of beer. Never a cold can. He liked his lager room temperature.

Mom would command me to talk to him. I'd go over. Grandpop would eyeball me, then turn his attention back to his beer. If we were going to have a conversation, he was going to be the one to initiate it, not me. And if he did grace me with some words of wisdom, I'd better not even think about weighing in.

The hell do you know. I have neckties older than you.

You going to let me finish the story, or what?

Mickey go get me another beer.

But now I had a captive audience.

Grandpop was unconscious in his hospital bed, hooked up to tubes and plastic bags that ran under and over the flimsy gown they'd dressed him in. The room was small and smelled like ammonia cut with lemons. His fingernails were too long, too yellow. A computer kept track of his heart.

There was so much I wanted to ask. The whole walk over there, the questions wouldn't stop.

There are stories about comatose people hearing what's going on around them. Maybe if I spoke out loud, Grandpop would actually hear me. Maybe he'd reach for a pen and paper, scribble out a few clues so that I would finally understand it all?

"Grandpop. It's me, Mickey. Can you hear me?"

He didn't respond. All I heard was beeping, like an eternal game of Pong was playing itself out in the corner of the room. After a few seconds Grandpop twitched slightly, but that could have been my imagination. I pulled a plastic chair closer to the bed so I could see him, face-to-face.

"I found those pills in your medicine cabinet, Grandpop. I accidentally took a few. They're not Tylenol, I know that much."

My grandfather's right hand twitched a little, one of his gnarled fingers tapping the side of an IV tube. His eyes were shut, but busy beneath their lids. Rolling fast.

Maybe he *could* hear me.

"Did you take them?"

No response.

"Did they send you back to 1972?"

No response.

"Is that why you never saw any of us the past few years? Have you been busy going to the—"

The door behind me suddenly opened and a nurse stormed in. She had frosted blond hair that was so severely spiked that if she were to jump up toward the ceiling, she'd probably stick. The nurse ignored me and attended to the machines monitoring my grandfather. I was a visitor, but so what? She had things to do, a shift to finish.

So I shut up for a while. My questions weren't exactly for the general public. *Oh, don't mind me. Just talking to my comatose grandfather about pill-popping and time travel.* I rested my face in my hands, pretending to pray or something.

The nurse tapped my shoulder.

"Hey. You want his things?"

"Things?"

"You know. His clothes. They're in a plastic bag in the closet over there."

Grandpop was in a coma; I don't think he'd mind if his clothes stayed unwashed for the time being. And I wasn't about to blow three or four of my last dollars on dry cleaning.

"Not now. Thanks."

She gave me a *whatever* look and left.

After a while, so did I. It's hard asking tough questions when you know you're not going to hear an answer. It's all buildup and no release.

Or maybe Grandpop could hear every word I was saying and decided that his only grandson had lost his damn mind.

I DIDN'T KNOW WHAT Grandpop was doing in the past. But suddenly I knew what *I* wanted.

I wanted to see my dad one last time.

I had an overwhelming, primal need to experience my father in the flesh—not in a photograph, not a memory. I wanted to see my father in real life, through my adult eyes. The older I got, and the greater the time since he'd been killed, the more I distrusted my memories. I had no idea what he really looked like. I didn't care if he couldn't see me, or that we couldn't talk. I just wanted to look at him.

An editor buddy of mine at the *City Press*—a news editor named Tommy Piccolo—once told me that he'd lost his dad when he was young, too. We were in the bar across the street, drinking many, many beers, and had reached that place where we were feeling mutually nostalgic and depressed. Tommy's dad died when he was twelve years old, and now he was starting to doubt his own memories of the man.

"I mean, this was thirty-six years ago. I can't tell what's real in my mind, or what I've made up. I can't even hear his voice in my head. I imagine him talking to me and I think he's speaking in a voice I made up."

I told Tommy I knew exactly how he felt. And then I think I ordered us shots of whiskey.

But now I had a second chance. Who receives a gift like this and pushes it away?

I'd even be satisfied if this were an elaborate dream brought on by hallucinogenic drugs in pill form. It was better than the alternative. Which was nothing.

So on the walk back from the hospital, I made my decision. I would pop some little white pills and go back to Darrah Street in 1972 and break into my own childhood home. Maybe I'd bust a window, or throw a rock at the door . . . or wait. I didn't even have to break in. I could just knock something over in the backyard. That was the easiest way. There was an alley that led behind the row of houses on our block. I grew up playing in it, even though it was mostly overgrown with weeds, and the slabs of concrete had slowly chipped and shattered, letting the earth beneath reclaim its turf. I used to pretend it was a superhighway behind our house, and my toy cars could take me anywhere I wanted.

That's what I would do. Walk up the alley, leap the three-foot-tall rusted metal fence, then find something in the backyard to knock over. I remember my parents kept a small charcoal grill back there when I was growing up. That would be easy to tip.

Then he'd come out, and then I would see him.

All I wanted to do was see him one last time.

IF I WAS GOING to start wandering the past, I was going to need protection. I stuck to nights, so daylight wasn't an issue. But streetlights and ordinary household lamps hurt. Someone swings a flashlight the wrong way, it could potentially decapitate me. So I ransacked my grandpop's closet.

Every square inch of it was stuffed with button-down shirts and trousers, suit jackets, windbreakers, as well as plastic shopping bags full of ski caps, gloves and socks. It looked like a thrift store had gotten drunk and thrown up in here. Nails had been tapped into one wall, and over them hung cracked leather belts, suspenders and ties so loud they could blind the naked eye. And more boxes full of papers were piled up on the floor of the closet, as if he didn't have enough things strewn around the apartment. Sometimes I thought I didn't so much as move into Grandpop's apartment as his storage facility.

I pulled on the hangers, trying to separate the clothes for a better look. They seemed to belong to no particular decade. They were old man clothes now; they would have been old man clothes thirty or sixty years ago.

At least my own wardrobe was consistent. At the *City Press*, T-shirt and jeans were the order of the day. If I had to seek an audience with the mayor or a member of City Council, sure, I'd put on a shirt with buttons. I owned exactly one pair of black dress pants from God knows when, one navy blazer, and one pair of non-sneaker shoes—black slip-on Sketchers.

After about twenty minutes of pushing and searching, I found a tan overcoat in Grandpop's closet—the one men's accessory that never seemed to go completely out of style. Like a beard, an overcoat could cover any number of sins.

And it would protect about 90 percent of my body from exposure to the light.

Grandpop also had a battered fedora hanging on a nail. I laughed when I first saw it. But light protection is light protection. And considering that one beam of light could potentially give me a lobotomy, it seemed like a smart thing to wear in the past.

It fit, too.

DUSK FELL. IT WAS time. I was buttoned up my shirt and fastened the belt on the overcoat. I tried to do that thing where you roll your hat down your arm, Gene Kelly style, but it just slipped off and floated to the ground.

I took three pills then laid down on the couch, overcoat wrapped around my body, gloves on my hand, fedora on my head—even though the apartment was sweltering. I tried to relax, let the pills do their job. Question was, would the coat, gloves and hat still be on my other body when I woke up?

My eyelids closed and then a second later I was back in 1972. And the hat, coat and gloves were still on. I checked the bathroom mirror, even lifting the hat from my head to make sure it wouldn't vanish on me. But I was afraid to let go. Maybe if contact were broken it would fade away, like the ring and pinky finger of my left hand. I didn't want to lose the hat just minutes after I'd found it.

IN THE PAST THE office was empty. DeMeo had gone off to wherever he hung his cock at night. And the front door was locked.

Fortunately the tumble lock worked from the inside, so all I had to do was flip the latch and twist the doorknob. But with my other self, simple tasks took on a new and startling complexity. I flipped the latch, but I was unable to grab hold of the knob. The moment I had the knob, the latch would slip out of my three remaining fingers. And . . . repeat.

A few minutes later I finally made it out the front door. Halfway down the staircase I heard a shrill laugh, like someone was being tickled to the point of death. I was wrong. It wasn't a laugh. It was a scream—a child's scream.

Coming from 2-C.

Then there was a sickening thud as something hit the wall right next to the door, so hard I felt the entire hall shake around me. There was another cry followed by something sharp—a slap. Another thud against the wall, then a *please please please Mom no.*

Goddammit I told you to be a quiet!

This was none of my business. I knew that. What happened behind closed doors should stay behind—

Oh screw that.

I raced to the door and tried the handle. Locked. I guess if you're going to beat your son you're going to want to bolt your front door for privacy.

So I made a fist and pounded it into the door five times quickly, hard as I could. The crying choked off into a startled gasp. I heard a *shhhhh.* Footsteps approached the door. There was a hushed *Shut up! Now! I mean it!* Then a snuffle and a cough. The lock tumbled, the door creaked open. Erna, the woman from DeMeo's office upstairs, peered out into the hallway. Mascara was running down the sides of her cheeks. Her skin was flush, hair askew. She couldn't see me of course.

"Is someone there?"

"Yeah, Erna. It's me. How about you stop smacking your kid."

"Hello?"

I doubt if I would have been so bold in real life. But here, my *other self* was invisible. Nobody could hear my words—except maybe the kid. And that's what I was counting on. To make sure he knew someone was listening. That his abuse was not going unnoticed.

Erna looked around the hallway again, then took a step back and started to close the door. But before it shut completely, she looked directly into my eyes. It wasn't a momentary gaze—our eyes meeting by accident. I swear, for a second there, *she saw me*.

Then she slammed the door shut.

I stayed outside the door for a while, listening for the slaps or the crying to resume. If it did, I would pound on the door again. I could do this all night, or until the pills ran out, whichever came first. But 2-C remained silent. Soon I felt awkward, standing in a dark hallway in 1972. So I put my ear to the door one last time, heard nothing but silence, and continued down the stairs to Frankford Avenue.

IT WAS BITTER COLD outside. Traffic crawled down the avenue. The El rumbled overhead, bringing home workers from downtown. The frigid air felt good in my other lungs.

I wasn't quite ready to go to Darrah Street yet, so I wandered across the street to the newsstand. A headline on the cover of the *Evening Bulletin* caught my eye:

4 Y.O. GIRL MISSING

Standing belly-to-counter at the newsstand—hoping nobody would bump into me and/or *through* me—I skimmed the story.

The words were tough to read in the near-dark, and there were just a few inches of copy before the jump, but it was enough to get the idea. A four-year-old girl named Patty Glenhart had gone missing from Kresge's, just a few blocks from where I stood.

At first I was filled with that sick feeling you get when you read about something tragic like this. You wish this didn't have to happen. Then my self-defense system kicked in. Push it away, because there was nothing I could do about it except send thoughts and prayers to the little girl's fam—

And then I remember where I was, *when* I was.

I *could* do something.

VII

THE PIT

I NEEDED A COPY OF the paper. I needed details. Names, addresses. Reporter stuff. Another fumbling routine later—this one lasting a full half-minute—I had a copy of the *Evening Bulletin* tucked under my arm.

Back upstairs in the office I opened the paper and memorized as much as I could. The Glenhart family lived on Allengrove Street in Northwood, about six blocks away. Patty had two older brothers, both in school. The girl, even though she was barely out of toddlerhood, was incredibly precocious. According to her mother, she had the habit of marching up to the Kresge's luncheonette counter and ordering something to eat before her mother could say otherwise. The waitress and cook thought it was cute, and usually gave her a free snack.

But the same waitress and cook were quoted as noticing some "creepy" guy with long sideburns and a yellow jacket lurking near the lunch counter around the same time the mother started screaming for help, where's my baby, oh God, where's my baby. Police are seeking all leads, please call MU6-8989 . . .

I read as much I could, committing as many details as possible to memory, then laid down on the floor and waited until I felt the familiar dizzy feeling again. I had taken four pills. I thought I would need the time, stalking my own father. I hadn't counted on this.

After a while I must have fallen asleep because the next thing I knew I was back in the apartment.

AFTER PULLING MYSELF UP off the floor I checked the time on my laptop—3:17 a.m. Only a few hours until sunrise. Not much time at all left.

I hit Google and typed in "Glenhart" and "Allengrove" and "missing" and I got a hit immediately.

LIKE EVERY OLD CITY, Philadelphia has a long history of atrocities. Some made national headlines, like Gary Heidnick and his in-famous West Philly basement of sex slaves. Or the shooting of a police officer by a radio journalist who would later receive the death penalty and become a cause célèbre. Or the 1985 bombing of an entire city block to combat a bunch of radicals who called themselves Move. Only, that last one was the fault of the mayor.

But even here in Northeast Philadelphia—for which Frankford served as an unofficial border between it and the rest of the city—there were plenty of atrocities, too.

Take the "Boy in the Box"—the name given to a kid, no more than six years old, who was found beaten to death and dumped in an old J.C.Penney bassinet box along the side of a quiet street back in 1957. Despite intense publicity, and a photo of the boy included in every city gas bill, his identity remains unknown to this day.

Closer still was the Frankford Slasher, a serial killer who preyed on prostitutes in Frankford during the late 1980s. I hadn't been kidding with Meghan about that; the Slasher was real. Police apprehended a man who was later convicted of one of the murders, but the real Slasher is believed to be dead or still at large.

This wasn't the case with "The Girl in the Pit," another Frankford atrocity. I was surprised that I'd never heard of it. I made it a point to seek out any crime stories that took place where I grew up.

But one amateur true-crime website had posted a quick case summary. The story was real. Patty Glenhart had gone missing, and stayed missing. They found her body years later.

I didn't linger over gruesome details. I only cared about two things: the name of the bastard who had taken her.

And his address.

THE HOUSE WAS A single on Harrison Street, just four blocks away from where I grew up. It dwarfed much of the other homes in the area, and had a wide skirting of lawn on both sides. A deep porch. Three floors, including an attic.

The top floors didn't interest me—it was the pit. It was little more than a crawl space under the laundry room just behind the kitchen. But according to the website, the pit was where the remains of Patty Glenhart were discovered by a new owner doing renovations. There was a full, unfinished basement in this house, but the pit was something extra, hand-dug by the previous owner. The killer of Patty Glenhart.

His name was Dennis Michael Vincent. After his arrest in October 1983, Vincent admitted to police that he intended it as a bomb shelter in case the Russians had any H-bombs pointed at Frankford. He'd grabbed four-year-old Patty because he thought an attack was coming in March 1972 and he wanted to save her because she was so blond and young and beautiful and would be useful when it came time to repopulate the country. Forensic investigators would find twenty-seven of her bones broken, and her head fractured in six places.

Later, Vincent claimed he'd been mistaken. She wasn't beautiful. She was evil. She was the daughter of the devil.

So now I stood in front of Vincent's house, wondering how to break in. The front door was locked. So were the windows. I moved along the side of the house and climbed onto the wooden porch. There was still a summer weather screen on the back door. Vincent hadn't bothered to change it out, even though it was February. I pressed the fingers of my right hand into the mesh screen and clawed down as hard as I could. The material slipped beneath my fingers. I clawed harder, hanging as much weight as I could on it.

The screen ripped a little. I put three fingers into the hole and tore it away from the frame.

There was an eye latch and hook. I worked it free, then tried the handle of the storm door.

It was locked.

But the door was wooden, with a single pane of built-in glass. I stepped back down to the yard, found a rock, then tapped it against the glass. It held. I couldn't risk smashing it too hard—I had to be quiet here. Stealthy. I tapped the rock again. The glass splintered a little. A few taps later it finally broke, the shards clinking on the linoleum floor on the other side.

I waited.

No sound, no nothing. It was close to four in the morning.

I pushed away the rest of the glass then reached my arm in to flip the latch. This took me a long time, especially since I couldn't see what the hell I was doing. Ghosts in movies have it easy. They can walk through walls, float up through a ceiling, sink down into the floor, whatever. Here I was, having trouble with the most rudimentary door lock ever created.

Finally the lock opened, but there was another one. A deadbolt. Hadn't counted on that. I reached my arm in farther and wrapped my fingers around the nub and pulled hard. It moved a fraction of an inch. I pulled again. It opened with a loud clack.

I was in.

Now I needed to find that laundry room and the pit beneath. I prayed I wasn't too late. Prayed that Vincent the monster hadn't taken her and killed her in the same day.

The time was 11:00 p.m. according to a cuckoo clock in Vincent's kitchen. The whole place was full of dusty antique furniture, which made me think Vincent's parents had been well-to-do but died young, and left him a ton of things he didn't know what to do with. Including adulthood.

Did he sleep upstairs? Or did he keep vigil by the trapdoor he'd jerry-rigged on the wooden floor of the laundry room?

I kept moving.

The laundry room wasn't hard to find. It was right behind the kitchen, and I could see the hand-sawed square in the floor, with the rusty hinges on one side and a deadbolt handle on the other. Yes, more locks. It took me a full minute to work it free and jump down into the dark pit.

My mouth instantly tasted like dirt. I pressed my hands against the floor and pushed up, spitting and snuffing. It was freezing down here. There was about four feet of space below the boards, with a wildly uneven muddy brown floor carved out. The dirt was cold and clammy under my palms, and felt like greasy modeling clay.

There was almost no light down here, but I could make out a few things the more my eyes adjusted. On one side was a small kid-sized mattress. No bed frame, just a single sheet that half-covered a cheap mattress that looked shiny. In a cardboard box next to the mattress were a couple of toys—a worn fabric doll, a wooden

duck with red wheels and a string attached to its beak. The kind of toys you expect to find in an orphanage. A badly run, broke-ass orphanage.

And curled up in a corner was Patty Glenhart.

She was sleeping on the dirt next to an exposed pipe. Condensation dripped from the rusted metal. She must have chosen that spot because it was slightly warm. I moved closer then whispered to her, not wanting to frighten her more than she already was.

"Patty."

She groaned. Curled up tighter into herself.

"I'm going to get you out of here, Patty, I promise. You'll be back with your mommy and daddy soon."

From behind a small forearm covered with light, downy hair, a tiny eye forced itself open. A beautiful green eye.

And then she screamed.

I tried shushing her, reassuring her, but it was too late. Her piercing cry traveled up the pipes, through the floorboards, through everything, and convinced Dennis Michael Vincent—who was probably already awake, sitting in his parents' old king-sized bed on the second floor—that something was wrong. I heard his heavy footsteps clomping down a wooden staircase. He was coming down to check on his captive.

"Patty! Listen to me! You need to be quiet!"

Then he was right above us, almost tripping over the open trapdoor.

"The *hell*!?"

Years from now, the neighbors would come forward with all kinds of details. Like how they remembered Vincent putting out ten paper bags of dirt for each weekly garbage collection. Didn't even dump the dirt in the backyard; he put it out for the trash guys to pick up. Neighbors would also remember hearing sawing and hammering—and, once in a while, screaming. But they just thought it was a cowboy or science fiction show on TV. Maybe a war picture. Nothing to worry about.

Couldn't they hear Patty's screams now? Why didn't they pick up the telephone and call the police—if nothing else but to put their minds at ease?

There was a harsh, bright light from above as Vincent turned on a light in the laundry room. Instantly I felt like I was going to throw up. The light again. Light did not like me. I inched backwards, trying to tuck myself back into the shadows. Of all of the Achilles' heels in the world to have, why did mine have to be the thing the planet is bathed in half the time? And could be summoned with the flick of a switch?

Two brown work boots landed on the dirt, along with two legs clad in muddy denim. Then his whole form crouched down. Dennis Michael Vincent was a tall man. Ruddy-cheeked, big-boned with sideburns gone wild. His eyes were too close together, like he'd grown up while the upper half of his face stayed frozen.

"Shhhh now little girl," he said. "We talked about this now. You don't want to get the belt again do you? You want me to bring the belt into the pit?"

I lunged at him.

IT HURT LIKE HELL—my *other* bones colliding with his real ones. But I think it hurt Vincent, too. And confused him. He grunted and spun around, squinting into the near darkness. I hissed at him, trying to sound as monstrous as possible.

"Get out of here now."

Let him worry. Let him freak. Let him run screaming from his own house. Maybe then the neighbors would do something.

"Who is that? What the—"

I didn't know if he could hear me. I didn't care. It made me feel good.

"I'm the Devil. I'm here for my daughter."

I charged him again.

This time, though, Vincent managed to grab me for a few seconds—how, I have no idea. But the light from above burned my back. I felt like I was going to throw up and fry to death at the same time. I twisted and rolled across the dirt, hearing Patty's screams and Vincent's fevered grunts as he searched for whatever was attacking him.

The opposite corner of the pit was pitch dark. I crouched there for a moment, trying to catch my breath and fight the dizziness I was feeling. Not yet. I couldn't wake up just yet. Just a little while longer. Just until she's free.

"You're doing that, aren't you? You're doing that, aren't you, you little whore?"

Patty screamed, but the cry was broken in half, like she'd been throttled halfway through.

"You're doing that because you're the daughter of the Devil! You stop it! You stop it or I'll use the belt on you until your bottom bleeds!"

There was a slap. I charged him again. I didn't care if I burned alive down there. I needed this man to *stop hurting this child.*

Vincent's head struck pipe. There was a dull bonging sound and a second later he cried out in agony. Then he went scrambling up out of the pit. I grabbed a sheet from the kiddie mattress, draped it over my head and then climbed up into the laundry room, not stopping until I was safe in the darkness of the living room. He was in there, too. I could make out his dim form among the shadows, mouth agape, eyes bulging, trying to figure out what the hell was chasing him.

"I'm still here."

I snarled, then smacked a lamp off a table.

Vincent screamed, stepped backwards.

I moved in closer, looking at his body, wondering where I could strike that would do the most damage.

"Go outside. Call to your neighbors for help. Tell them to send the police. Tell them the Devil has come for you."

Vincent stumbled backwards until he bumped into his living room wall. He was panting. Shaking his head.

And then he reached over and flicked on the living room lights.

I THREW MY RIGHT arm up in the air. For a moment I must have looked like one of the scenes from 1950s movies about people caught in the flash of an H-bomb explosion. As if a forearm and bicep can hold back sheer atomic hell? I didn't black out, but I think I stopped recording conscious memories, because the next thing I knew I was huddled beneath a coffee table. Vincent was taunting me:

"Devil don't like the light, does he?"

My right arm was paralyzed by agony. Physical pain is one thing. As bad as it gets—like, say, *torture room* bad—you can always go into shock and retreat inside yourself. For whatever reason, this felt like *soul pain* . . . pain you couldn't hide from, *ever*. So long as your soul exists.

I couldn't take it anymore so I darted for the only available darkness—the kitchen. Then under the table. Sliding across the linoleum. Shaking badly. Ready to throw up and pass out.

"I'll give you light, Devil!"

Another click. More light, all around me. Where the hell was I? Right. Kitchen. There was cool linoleum beneath my fingers—the remaining fingers of my left hand, that is. I didn't know where my right hand was.

Two brown work boots appeared in front of me. The table above me began sliding to the left. Then two table legs lifted up from the floor. The shadow line raced toward me. And with it, a wave of murderous light. It was endgame time.

So I charged at the son of a bitch with all of my remaining strength.

Momentum propelled me forward, forward, forward. There was a crashing sound and I felt like I'd tumbled into a Black & Decker food processor. Skin, shredded; bones, ground to dust. Nerves, sliced open and prodded with hot needles.

But somehow I was still alive.

And in the cool, soothing darkness of night once again.

Dennis Michael Vincent lay next to me, gurgling, on the concrete path on the side of his house. We had gone through the kitchen window, and now pieces of glass were sticking out of his neck and forearms. Blood squirted from the right side of his throat in small, urgent beats. He moaned. Cursed the devil with the little bit of voice he had left.

There was a burst of yellow light to my right. The sound of a wooden door creaking open. A neighbor.

I crawled backwards until I felt a metal chain-link fence behind me. I tried to use it to stand up, but something weird was happening. I couldn't seem to grab hold of anything. I heard a noise, then looked back at the house.

Patty Glenhart was standing on the back porch. She saw me. I guess only kids and psychos could see ghosts.

She screamed and turned and ran back into the house.

I glanced down at my right shoulder. My arm was completely gone.

The neighbors next door were calling out. *Is everybody okay? Does anyone need help?*

Meanwhile, Dennis Michael Vincent choked on his own blood.

I tried to forget my missing arm and used the three fingers on my left hand to pull myself up the fence until I was standing. Then I staggered along the side of the house, completely thrown off-balance. I turned right and walked a block, trying to make it to Frankford Avenue before I passed out.

WHEN I WOKE UP Meghan was staring at me. She had a cell phone in her hand and a panicked expression on her face. I was on the floor, wrapped in Grandpop's overcoat, his fedora still on my head.

"Christ, Mickey—are you awake?"

"Oh God."

I groaned, then rolled over on my side, wondering what Meghan was doing here. Wondering how I was going to explain why I was dressed in a coat, hat and gloves on the floor on a sweltering June morning.

"Mickey! Come on, stop screwing around!"

My right arm was still attached to my body, but like the fingers on my left hand, it was completely numb. A useless slab of dead meat hanging from my shoulder. Fingers were one thing. A whole arm was something else.

The pain coursing through my body was unreal. It was like the flu on anabolic steroids.

"I'm one button away from 911 unless you tell me what's going on. And this time, I'm going to make sure they pump your stomach."

I looked at her. Swallowed.

"I'm not . . . I'm not on drugs. I swear. Just help me up and bring over my laptop."

"What? Your laptop? Why?"

"It's important. *Please.*"

Against her better judgment, Meghan put the phone down and helped me to the houndstooth couch, then grabbed my laptop from the cherrywood desk and put it on my lap. I used my three good fingers to pull it into a useful typing position.

"Hey—what's wrong with your arm?"

"It's numb. Hang on a minute."

It was difficult to type with three fingers. I knew plenty of people got by with two, but you have to understand—I was hardwired to type with at least eight. (The pinky fingers usually sit out my work sessions, like foremen on a construction crew.) Using three was unnatural. Using three was like trying to put in a contact lens using my elbows.

"Want me to do that for you?"

"I got it."

I hunt-and-pecked "Patty Glenhart" and looked for the entry I'd found earlier.

It was gone.

I tried searching for it a different way, going to the main page of the true-crime website (SinnersAndSadists.com, it was called— charming, huh?) and search by "W" and "P," but there was no entry about a girl named Patty Glenhart.

Meghan touched my shoulder.

"What are you looking for?"

"Hopefully, something that isn't there."

It sounded absurd, but maybe I'd actually gone back and changed things. Maybe there was a little girl who was alive right now because I traveled back to the year 1972 and pushed a pedophile out of his kitchen window. I'd lost the use of my arm in the process, but that didn't matter, because maybe, just maybe Patty Glenhart was alive and the bad dreams were behind her.

Meghan looked at me.

"You know, for someone who's trying to convince me that they're not on drugs, you're doing a really awful job."

"Swear to God, I'm not on drugs."

"You're talking gibberish. I found you on the floor, wrapped in an overcoat and wearing a hat. Your right arm is numb. Tell me which of these things does not say, *I'm having a lost weekend in the middle of the week*. What's going on?"

There were a million reasons not to tell Meghan what was going on. The spiral of insanity I mentioned.

But I told her anyway.

AFTER I'D FINISHED LAYING it out for her—and I must have done a fairly good job, because she didn't interrupt once—Meghan asked me if I wanted some Vitamin Water. I told her sure. She removed a plastic bottle from a paper bag she'd placed on the cherrywood desk, unscrewed it, then handed it to me. I was clever enough not to reach for it with my right hand. But not clever enough to realize that my three-finger grip on the bottle wouldn't be enough. It slipped straight down, bouncing slightly on a couch cushion, and gushing pale purple liquid all over my lap.

"Gah!"

I lifted the laptop out of the way. It was a Mac relic, but it was also my only link to the outside world. That is to say, anyplace that wasn't Frankford.

"Shit, I'm sorry," Meghan said, picking up the bottle and then darting across the room in search of a clean towel. Which she wouldn't find, since I hadn't done laundry since I'd moved in. There were two paper towels left on a roll that my grandpop must have purchased. She brought them over, started patting my lap.

"Dear Penthouse Letters. I swear this never happened to me before, but one night . . ."

Meghan shot me a sardonic grin. It was the first joke we'd shared in days, and it felt nice. She finished soaking up what she could, then balled up the paper towels and executed a perfect hook into the sink. Then she grabbed my knees and looked me dead in the eye.

"Here's how this is going to work."

"How *what* is going to—"

"Don't interrupt me. I'm going to try to shoot holes in everything you've just told me. If it all holds up when we're finished, then I'll stay and we can talk through this. But if I get the slightest hint you're messing with my head, or inventing some bullshit story because you're out of your mind on drugs, then I'm gone."

"Okay."

"Last chance. You swear that everything you've told me is true?"

"Yes. To the best of my knowledge. Want me to put my numb right hand on a Bible?"

Meghan was her father's daughter. She wasn't a lawyer. In fact, I had no idea what she did for a living—if she made a living for herself at all. Our friendship had revolved around life in the Spruce Street apartment building, as well as its nearby bars and restaurants. But some of her father's prosecutorial skills must have rubbed off on her, because she grilled me like a pro.

First, she demanded to see these "pills." I told her to check the Tylenol bottle in the medicine cabinet. She found them, tapped one out into her hand. Examined it. Looked for a brand name, but couldn't find one. They were smooth white capsules with only the dosage (250 mg) carved along one side.

She placed the pill in a small Ziploc baggie like she was preserving the chain of evidence.

"What are you going to do with that?"

"Don't worry about it."

Next Meghan took me through my alleged physical interactions in the past. So I could open doors and walk downstairs, but I had trouble picking up newspapers and comic books? Why? Light hurt my body, but only direct light—is that correct? What about ambient light? When your fingers fell off, did they disappear right away, or after a few seconds?

"Okay, and you say no one can see you?"

"Almost nobody. That kid I mentioned."

"Whose name you don't know."

"Right. He can see me. And the little girl, Patty. I think she could see me."

"Hmmmm."

We went around and around this for a good half-hour until she finally circled back to Patty Glenhart. Meghan wouldn't let go of it.

"Your only proof was this profile on a blog."

"A true-crime website."

"Whatever. And when you searched for the profile, just now, it was gone, right?"

"Right."

"What if the site administrator just took it down?"

"You mean coincidentally, just a few hours after I first read it?"

"It's a possibility. Or, you could have hallucinated the entry."

I thought about this.

"Wait. There was that piece in the *Bulletin*, with the 'Girl Missing' headline."

"Do you have a copy?"

"No. I can't bring anything back, remember?"

"But this newspaper has to exist."

She turned away from me, as if making a mental note to herself.

"You say you went back and got her out of that basement, but you didn't prevent her abduction."

"Right!"

"I'll check the *Bulletin* morgue tomorrow. If you saw the headline, then it'll be there."

"You know about the *Bulletin* morgue?"

The morgue was part of Temple University's Urban Archives center, and was basically the clips files of the long-defunct newspaper. Before the Internet, if you wanted to look up a piece of Philadelphia history, you had to go to the morgue and look through dozens of tiny manila envelopes, each stuffed with little yellowed clippings, which had been cut by hand and dated by some longforgotten staffer. It was basically a steampunk version of Google, and it had been my secret reporting weapon for years.

But it was old news to Meghan.

"We went there freshman year. Our English professor took us on a field trip. Doesn't every college send their freshmen down there?"

Finally, Meghan turned her attention back to my numb arm and fingers, asking if I could wiggle them, or feel anything when she poked my forearm with a fork. Which she did. Repeatedly. Up and down my skin. But nothing.

"Okay, this is kind of scary. Let me take you to the hospital."

"No. I hate those places. Plus, I'm pretty sure I don't have health insurance."

"Even if I do believe your crazy ass story about the pills—and the jury's still out, by the way—why wouldn't you want to have your arm checked? You could have pinched a nerve. You could lose feeling in it forever."

"I just need to sleep. And what do you mean the jury's still out? Have you found a single hole in my story?"

"Not yet. But I haven't found any proof either."

I thought about it for a moment. Then it hit me.

"Okay then. I'll give you proof."

MEGHAN HELD THE STEAK knife with both hands, fingers on the handle and the dull edge of the blade. She looked up at me, pointed down at the pill. "Good enough?"

"No. Cut it again. I don't want to be out long."

"So an eighth, then? And let me repeat that this is a stupendously bad idea."

"Just cut the pill."

"For all we know, these pills are causing the numbness. And the hallucinations."

"They're not hallucinations."

Meghan handed me the tiny sliver of the pill anyway.

"You're an idiot."

"Right up there."

I pointed to the chipped wooden molding around the bathroom door. The molding was the same in 1972 as it was today. It hadn't even been painted, as far as I could tell.

"I'm going to go back and carve your initials into that molding."

"You're such a romantic."

Her initials were MC. Not long after I'd met Meghan and learned her last name was "Charles"—names didn't get more Main

Line than that—I started calling her MC Meghan, which not only failed to make literal sense, but also annoyed her to no end.

Meghan eyed the molding skeptically, even reaching up to brush it with her fingertips, as if I'd already carved her initials there, then covered it up with a generous helping of dust.

"Again for the record . . ."

"This is stupid, I know."

I popped the pill in my mouth then laid down on the couch.

"See you in a little while. Watch that doorway."

Dizziness. Head throbs. Weak limbs. Then my eyelids felt like they were a thousand pounds each.

I WOKE UP IN the office back in 1972. And yes, my right arm was gone, all the way up to the shoulder. I shouldn't have been surprised by this, but I was. And more than a little horrified. The missing limb really threw my balance off. I swear to God, I felt myself tilting to one side.

Plus, I'd have to do my initial-carving one-handed.

There was nothing sharper than a butter knife in the kitchenette drawer. Not the most ideal cutting tool. Carving those two letters might take me the entire trip back to the past, but so be it. I would love to be there, in the present, to watch Meghan's face when her initials start to carve themselves into the paint-chipped wood. Would they slowly appear, one stroke at a time? Or would she blink and then see all at once, the new reality conforming around her?

I wondered if Grandpop Henry, sometime down the road, would notice the initials and take a moment to ponder them.

The idea that I was about to change reality hit me hard. I'd read enough sci-fi novels growing up to know about the so-called butterfly effect—change one thing in the past, and the ripple effects could be potentially disastrous. Would something as simple as initials on a door frame make a difference? Sure, maybe if I carved a message like STAY OUT OF NYC ON 9-11-01 or BUY MICRO-SOFT. Initials were innocuous, though . . . right?

Then again, I had prevented a little girl's death a few hours ago. And now there was one more person in the world who previously hadn't been with us. Had someone died in her place? Had she grown up to do something awful? What havoc had I already wreaked?

I'd just pressed the tip of the knife to the molding when there was a loud scream outside my door.

The cry of a boy.

I KNEW I SHOULDN'T GO to the door. I should just proceed with my original plan and start carving Meghan Charles's initials into the wooden molding around my grandpop's bathroom door.

But you're only blessed with this kind of insight after the fact. After everything's been taken away from you, and it's too late to change a thing.

Instead, I walked across the room and pressed my ear to the pebbled glass.

I heard heavy footsteps.

There was the sound of slapping, and then another cry, and footsteps running down the hall. And then the gunshot slam of the door down on the ground floor. After a few minutes I managed to open the front door.

Bright sunshine. It was morning. The intensity of the light made me blink. My vision turned white. I dropped the butter knife. I slammed the door shut and crouched down and turned my back to the door and leaned against it and concentrated on breathing slowly.

I heard Erna's shrill voice filling the hallway:

"Listen to me! You have to be quiet! Do you want us to get kicked out of here? Thrown out on the street to live like animals?"

And then:

"Shut up shut up SHUT UP. Not another sound!"

And then finally:

"BILLY ALLEN DERACE YOU STOP CRYING OR I'LL GIVE YOU SOMETHING TO CRY ABOUT."

VIII

NO MORE MICKEY

BARELY HAD TIME TO process the name before that familiar dizzy feeling washed over me. No, no, not now. Not now! I slammed my fists into the wall, as if slamming my fists would help me stay there just a few seconds longer so I could think . . .

Billy Allen Derace? That twelve-year-old redheaded kid downstairs was going to grow up and stab my father to death?

Of course he was.

I WASN'T EVEN CONSCIOUS for two seconds before Meghan was leaning over me, whispering in my ear. Her breath was sweet and warm. I could feel sweat beading on my skin, my cheeks and forehead burning and the veins in my head throbbing.

"Hey genius, it didn't work."

The levels of exhaustion in my bones and muscles and head were unreal. Maybe I'd been overdoing the pills. Maybe the loss of sensation in my arm and fingers was just the beginning—a herald of things to come. Maybe Grandpop Henry had taken too many pills and ended up in his coma.

"Yeah."

I tried to roll over. After a moment or two, I gave up.

Much better to stay here on the floor. Let the sweat dry on my skin. Give the throbbing a chance to die down. Take a little more time to recover.

Meghan touched my forehead. I didn't want her to. My forehead was sweaty, gross, hot.

"Are you saying you *didn't* go back this time?"

"No, no . . . I did."

"Then what happened?"

I didn't want to answer any more questions. I didn't want to think about butterfly effects or proof or my numb arm or Patty Glenhart or Billy Allen Derace or any of it. I just wanted the throbbing and the sweating to stop. I just wanted sleep.

"Mickey Wade, will you please answer me?"

"No. I won't. You should go."

"Hey, what's wrong?"

"Just please go away. I need to rest."

Hurt flashed in her eyes, only to be quickly erased and replaced with anger.

"Fine," she said, and then a few seconds later I heard my apartment door slam. And a little while after that, the Frankford El thundered by, rolling into the station. Somehow I crawled up to the houndstooth couch, using only one arm. I curled up best I could, trying not to think about the cushion that was still damp with Vitamin Water, trying not to think about anything.

Except the one thing I couldn't help thinking about.

Billy Allen Derace.

I SLEPT SO LONG that it was evening again before I woke up. And I was still stupid with exhaustion. At least the throbbing in my head was almost gone, and the sweat had cooled and dried on my skin. On the downside, my right arm was still useless. Numb. Dead.

I fished an old scarf out of a plastic bag in Grandpop's closet, then used it to make a lame sling for my right arm, just so it wouldn't be hanging next to my body, flopping around as I moved. I thought about using some of my remaining cash on a proper sling. But beer was a cheaper fix. Maybe tomorrow.

The El rumbled past my windows, came to a grinding stop at the station, bringing commuters home from work. But very few of them would be climbing off the train and walking to their homes in Frankford. They would be walking down the stairs and hoping to catch the 59 or the K at the mini-terminal up Arrott Street, where they'd be transported to safer parts of near Northeast Philly. Or they'd be riding the El down to the end of the line, Bridge and Pratt, just ten blocks away, where they'd take buses to the upper Northeast or suburbs. They wouldn't linger in Frankford any longer than they had to. Their parents may have stopped to browse some of the shops along the avenue, but those days were gone now.

I ate a plate of apples and had a few spoonfuls of peanut butter for dessert. I finished off four cans of Golden Anniversary and didn't feel a thing.

My mom had called three times today. The first two messages were the same litany—*how's the job hunt, did you visit your grandfather, we'd really like you to come to dinner soon.* The third however, was different.

Mickey, your grandfather's awake.

GRANDPOP WAS STARING AT me.

His eyes would focus for a moment, then turn away, as if he was too tired to maintain eye contact. Then they'd roll, and he'd move his tongue around his dry mouth like he was preparing to speak. But no words came out. He couldn't move his arms or legs. The only movements were in his eyes and lungs—gently inflating and pushing up against his ribs, and then deflating a moment later.

"Hi, Grandpop."

The old man focused on me for a brief moment, and then his eyes rolled elsewhere.

My mom was in the room with us. She'd left work early that afternoon when she received the call from the hospital, and waited here until I showed up. Now it was my turn, she said.

Turn for what, exactly?

There was little love lost between my mother and her father-in-law. She felt obligated to invite him to family events—and my grandpop almost always accepted, perhaps out of the same, misguided sense of obligation. But they rarely spoke, except to say "Merry Christmas" or "Yeah, Happy Easter" or my grandpop to ask where my mom was keeping the beer, or my mom to ask Grandpop if he wanted more potato salad. Sometimes I thought she kept up the charade for my benefit, that I shouldn't be deprived of my Wadcheck heritage.

She reached out to hug me.

"Why don't you come for dinner later?"

I only half-hugged her back—mainly because I had shoved my dead right hand into my jeans pocket. Letting it hang loose would be suspicious, and putting it up in my scarf sling would seal the deal. Mom would frog-march me down to the ER in seconds.

"We'll see."

"We have to talk, Mickey. About your grandfather. And what to do with him."

He was staring at us.

"Mom, he's right here, you know."

"I know that. Anyway, try for six. You can just walk up Oxford . . ."

"I know where you live."

"Funny, you don't act like it."

"Yeah, Mom. Bye."

Another five minutes passed before I'd worked up the courage to start asking questions. Grandpop, limited to eye contact, seemed to encourage me. He'd shoot me a stare, as if to say *Well, get on with it* before giving up and rolling his eyes and taking another labored breath.

"Grandpop, I found the pills."

This got his attention. Dead stare.

"I've used the pills. I've walked around in the past, just like you must have."

Dead stare.

"I also looked through your papers and found the files about my dad."

Dead stare.

"I also know who used to live downstairs."

That finally provoked a reaction. Grandpop's eyes narrowed. His mouth moved like he was trying to pry a piece of bread from the roof of his mouth, but he couldn't.

"What were you trying to do? Were you trying to prevent dad's murder?"

Grandpop's chest rose more quickly now. His eyes darted to the door, then back to me. He opened them wide, and then they rolled away again, like he was lost in exhaustion.

"What were you going to do?"

There was a rumbling in his throat now—an animal growl that started low and gradually increased in volume. His right hand trembled and began to close in a loose fist.

"Grandpop? I need to know what you were going to do."

His eyes opened again and locked on mine. His jaw dropped a fraction of an inch.

Then he slowly turned his head and there was nothing.

After another twenty minutes, I left the hospital and walked back to the apartment.

I'D HAD ENOUGH.

Enough of the pills. Enough of the calls. Enough of the past. I put the plastic bottle of pills back in the medicine cabinet and, after a few minutes of deliberation, I slipped the padlock through the steel eye on the medicine cabinet and snapped it shut.

There were more calls from my mom but I ignored them. No, I would not be joining my mom and her boyfriend for dinner in Northwood this evening. I would be staying home and dining on apples, peanut butter and a new six-pack of Golden Anniversary I'd purchased just for the occasion. Which pretty much broke the bank, but so what.

I'd had enough of the past.

The only music I had in the apartment was my father's old albums. My CD player was in storage, and the disk drive on my laptop was broken. But I didn't want to listen to any of my father's music. Nothing old. Not now.

The only books I owned were musty old crime paperbacks and collections of classic journalism—most of them picked up at that mystery bookstore on Chestnut Street. I used to walk in with twenty bucks, and the proprietor, Art, would send me out with a small shopping bag full of beat-up paperbacks. The appeal was simple: the novels acted like little portals into the past. I'd had enough of that to last me for a while.

The journalism and memoirs, too, were vintage: Hunter Thompson. Charles Bukowski. Joan Didion. John Gregory Dunne. Pete Dexter. Ancient history. Journalism was dying.

Everything around me was drowning in the past. The scrapbooks, full of old photos.

Like that scrapbook, full of images of my father as a soldier in Vietnam.

WHAT'S EMBARRASSING IS HOW little I know about my father's time there. I know he served two tours. I also know he volunteered for the army to avoid the draft—he was able to pick a better spot. My mother would make vague references to my dad shooting machine guns from helicopters and running through the jungle while tripping on acid. Then again, she also swore that my father had a secret Vietnamese half-family, and one day, they'd show up fresh from Saigon and demand to live in our house and eat our food.

It was the "eating our food" part that seemed to worry my mom the most.

I remember exactly one Vietnam War story, which came right from my father's lips. I was in the basement, and a cockroach skittered across my leg. I was about five. At that age, roaches terrified the shit out of me. I screamed and bolted upstairs, and my face smashed right into my father's hard belly. "Roach! Roach!" I was yelling.

"Hey, cool your tool," my dad told me. "Cockroaches are nothing. In the war we had scorpions, and they'd climb in your boots when you weren't looking. If you didn't shake them out of your boot, you were in trouble. One guy I knew stuck his foot inside his boot, turned white, then started yelling. He died a few minutes later."

That's my one Vietnam story.

Now that I thought about it, our longest conversations—consider that a euphemism—were about dying or death.

My first ever memory of my father was the two of us walking next to an in-ground pool. I must have been two or three years old. No idea where we were; nobody in family could afford a three-foot vinyl pool, let alone the in-ground version.

But the pool had a cover on it, weighed down with decorative stones at the edges. I must have started to walk near the pool, because my father's hand clamped down on my shoulder. Uh-uh, he'd said. You go in there, there'd be no more Mickey.

No more Mickey.

The best definition of death I'd ever heard.

I LAID BACK ON the couch and stared at the ceiling and did absolutely nothing except take a sip of beer every so often. I thought about my arm, and maybe the fact that I should have it checked out. This wasn't a joke; I had three functional fingers. What kind of job was I supposed to find where I could use only three fingers?

Maybe I could be a night watchman, just like my grandpop. Maybe that mental hospital would hire me. And then some weekend, maybe not too long from now, I would just stop working and check myself in.

I SWEAR I HEARD an audible *snap!* as the pieces fit together in my head.

LITERALLY, IT WAS IN the last box I checked. A collection of paystubs, bound together by a dirty and cracked rubber band.

Paystubs from the Adams Institute.

So *this* was the hospital where Grandpop had worked from about 1989 until he retired in 2003. A mental hospital.

No, not just a mental hospital. The *same* mental hospital where they kept Billy Derace, the man who witnesses say stabbed my father to death in a cheap dive.

My father. Grandpop Henry's son.

How had Grandpop been allowed to work there? Surely there had to be some kind of background check for security guards at the hospital. Then I looked down at the envelope and saw the name: Henryk Wadcheck. The world knew my murdered father as Anthony Wade. No connection there. And I'm sure Grandpop hadn't volunteered that information.

So was he just working there for the money? Or did he have a plot in mind?

Of course he had a plot in mind.

Because in 2002, he moved to the apartment *one flight up from where Billy Derace grew up.*

Because he had a locked medicine cabinet with a plastic bottle full of pills that would send him back in time.

Two events could be a coincidence. Not all of this.

And as I knelt in a messy pile of boxes and papers, there was a knock at my door.

MEGHAN DIDN'T SAY A word. She just walked in, placed a paper bag of groceries on the cherrywood desk. She glanced down at the mess on the floor, which, through her eyes, must have looked like I was building a wino-style nest for myself in the middle of the apartment. Then she reached into her oversized Kiplinger purse, pulled out a curled stack of papers and handed them to me.

"What's all this?"

Meghan looked at me.

"Patty Glenhart was real."

The top sheet was a photo of the original *Bulletin* story I'd first read back in 1972. "Girl Missing." Same lead, same byline, same story.

The next sheet, however, was her death notice.

"Wait—she *died*?"

"Keep reading."

The piece was from the *Philadelphia Inquirer*, and dated January 8, 1987. Patricia Anne Glenhart, twenty-seven years old, found beneath a truck two blocks from Frankford Avenue, wrapped in an old overcoat. She had been sexually assaulted, stabbed thirty-seven times.

"She's dead," I repeated.

"Yeah," Meghan said. "She has been for over twenty years now. Mickey, let me ask you something, and please don't mess around with my head. Please tell me the truth."

"Of course."

"The day you moved here, you were joking about somebody called the Frankford Slasher. Turns out he was real."

"I told you!"

"Do you know much about the case?"

"I grew up here, so I remember hearing a lot about it. But I also wrote a short follow-up piece for the *City Press* a few years ago. The murders are still unsolved, as far as the police are concerned."

"So you're familiar with the names of the victims."

Another snap in my head.

"Wait—Patty Glenhart was killed by the Frankford Slasher?"

Meghan nodded.

"But it was Patricia Bennett. Her married name. But her maiden name was Glenhart."

I flicked through the rest of the papers—which were *Inquirer* and *Daily News* accounts of the Slasher. Every article after January 1987 mentioned Patty Bennett. Meghan had highlighted the name in bright yellow.

The last piece was my own, from the *City Press*. It was titled "Under the El." There was a sidebar listing the fifteen known victims. In the middle of the list was Patty Bennett's name.

"No way."

"You wrote the piece, Mickey. Maybe you didn't consciously remember her name, or having read her maiden name somewhere, but your subconscious sure did. So when you started having your visions about saving some little girl, you dredged her up, and . . ."

"No. Not possible."

Of course I wrote the piece. I remembered agonizing over it, because I had a simple rule about writing first-person journalism pieces: namely, *don't*. But it had been the anniversary of the first Slasher victim, and I had been desperate to come up with something to fill a cover slot, and once my editor heard about it, she pretty much strong-armed me into making it a personal essay/follow-up piece. She had visions of state—maybe even national—awards; instead, it was more or less ignored except by certain Frankford business owners who called for a good month to complain.

THE VICTIMS OF THE Frankford Slasher were considered "nobodies"—female barflies, active or retired prostitutes, or other lost souls. They hopped bars—mostly Goldie's at Pratt Street, sometimes the Happy Tap closer to Margaret Street.

The Slasher was a few years into his work before anyone noticed the pattern. First was fifty-two-year-old Maggie Childs, who lived

WENDY SIMMONS

TERRY CONROY

MAGGIE CHILD

JAN WHITE

CAROL STRAUSS

JANET BAZELL

PETTIT

CAROL JOYCE

PATTY

in Oreland, a town in Montgomery County, but was reportedly a Goldie's regular, estranged from her husband. Her body was discovered in August 1985. Just five months later, the body of sixty-eight-year-old Carol Joyce was found on her bedroom floor, naked from the waist down, and stabbed six times, with the murder weapon still lodged in her torso. Joyce lived in South Philly, but was also a Goldie's regular. So was sixty-four-year-old Edie Pettit, who was found stabbed to death Christmas Day 1986. Just a few weeks later, in January 1987, twenty-eight-year-old Jan White, a former go-go dancer and homeless woman who slept on the street near Goldie's, was found beneath a truck near Dyre Street. She had been sexually assaulted, stabbed forty-seven times, and wrapped in an overcoat.

Neighbors soon put pressure on the police to catch the madman responsible for the killings.

Well over a year passed before sixty-six-year-old Janet Bazell was found stabbed to death in the vestibule of her apartment building on Penn Street near Harrison. She had been out drinking in the bars under the El, trying to forget the fact that she'd been evicted from her apartment that same day, November 11, 1988. Then, on January 19, 1989, Terry Conroy, thirty, was found in *her* apartment on Arrott Street, just above Griscom, cut to ribbons and wearing nothing but a pair of socks.

Witnesses started to come forward; Bazell and Conroy had been seen hanging out with a young white man, barely in his twenties. Sketches were made, circulated. No arrests came of them.

With the seventh murder came a break in the case. Carol Strauss, a forty-six-year-old woman with a history of mental illness, was found stabbed thirty-six times behind a seafood shop early in the morning of April 28, 1989.

The next morning, detectives questioned a shop employee

named Tyrell "Cooker" Beaumont, who casually told a friend in a bar that he knew one of the Frankford Slasher's previous victims. He also said he was with his girlfriend in his apartment the night of April 27, and both had seen a thin young white man with red hair lurking around the seafood store.

The only problem: Beaumont's girlfriend denied being with him that night. Two eyewitnesses, both prostitutes, placed Beaumont at the scene of the crime, with a large utility knife tucked in his belt, right around the time of the murders. To make matters worse, Shauyi Tan, Beaumont's former employer at the seafood shop, testified that he had told her, "Yeah, maybe I killed her." Then, a moment later, recanted. He was arrested a day later.

Despite the fact that previous eyewitnesses tagged the Frankford Slasher as a young redheaded white dude (Beaumont was African-American), many locals breathed a sigh of relief. *They caught the guy.*

Then came the murder of thirty-eight-year-old Wendy Simons, stabbed twenty-three times, and found in her Arrott Street apartment, just blocks away. Beaumont was in jail, awaiting trial, at the time.

Beaumont was tried and convicted of the murder of Carol Strauss in December 1990, based solely on eyewitness accounts. He was not tried for the other Frankford Slasher murders. Technically, those seven other murders—eight, including Patty Glenhart—are still unsolved. Whether the Wendy Simons murder was a copycat killer, or the real Frankford Slasher, remains unknown. "I was railroaded," Beaumont said after hearing the verdict. "I didn't kill Carol Strauss. I did not even know Carol Strauss. I was implicated by prostitutes, that is, pipers, that the police put up."

I THOUGHT I REMEMBERED the facts of the case fairly well; it had been a big deal to me when it finally appeared. It was the kind of story that made me want to be a journalist.

But now I looked at the sidebar again, did a quick count and saw there were fifteen victims.

No. That couldn't be right. When I wrote this piece, it was only nine.

I swear to God it had been only nine.

Fifteen was an absurdly high number. Did Gary Heidnick have that many victims? Did most serial killers?

"I think you need to see someone. My dad knows someone who would talk to you, keep it discreet."

"I'm not crazy."

"I know that, Mickey. I just think you've been living in your head too much lately. You need some help climbing out of it."

Did I make this stuff up? Was my subconscious mind putting on one hell of a show for me whenever I nodded off to sleep? When you look at it from the outside, from the other side of the glass, there was a compelling case for insanity. Only I was experiencing these things. Only I had proof. It could all be happening in my head, like Meghan said.

But I knew it wasn't. It was real. Senses don't lie. Not like this.

Meghan touched my shoulder.

"There's also the pill."

"What *about* the pill?"

"I have a friend who works for a drug company. One of the big ones. As a favor, he ran a few tests on the pill you gave me."

"You did what? Oh crap, Meghan. Why did you do that? You have no idea where it came from, and what it was . . ."

"Neither did you. And you popped it in your mouth."

"I thought it was Tylenol."

"The first time. But you kept taking it, even though you had no idea what it might be."

"Okay, good point."

"Thank you."

There was a quiet Old West–style standoff moment. She was waiting for me to draw, I believe, so she could expertly shoot the pistol out of my hand before twirling her own gun and replacing it smoothly in her holster. But I wasn't going to give her the satisfaction. She'd have to speak first. And she did.

"Do you want to know what the pill contained?"

"Sure."

"Nothing but sugar. It was a placebo. Meant for use as a control in pharmaceutical studies. Dan sees them all the time. Took him about five minutes to figure it out."

"Right. Which just goes to prove my main point that I am not on drugs. I may be on cheap beer, I might be a junkie when it comes to peanut butter and apples, but I'm not on drugs."

Meghan squinted.

"Peanut butter? Is that why your skin has this strange jaundiced tinge to it?"

"I also haven't been out of the apartment in a while."

"Anyway, that doesn't prove you're not on drugs. It just proves you're not on *those particular* drugs, because they're nothing but sugar."

"Jesus H. Christ on a stick. You moved me in! Did you see a box marked random drug paraphernalia? Did you see a bunch of syringes come tumbling out of an old shoe box?"

"What . . . you think I'd go through your things?"

"You told me yourself: you're a snoop."

"Touché."

I used the few moments of silence to run Meghan's evidence through the tired and confused computer encased inside my skull. Let's say she's right. The pills do jack shit. They're nothing but sugar. I was having ridiculously vivid dreams of wandering the streets of Frankford in the early 1970s all on my own. Patty Glenhart's story had been lurking in my subconscious for years now, waiting for the right dream/hallucination. And maybe it was the same thing with Billy Derace. Clearly I needed some kind of closure, so my brain supplied it. Just like I did with my college essay freshman year.

Wait.

I looked at Meghan.

"I'll be right back."

THE NAME ON THE downstairs mailbox for apartment 2-C was HYND, not DERACE. It had been scrawled on a paper mailing label, not a plastic strip with white punched letters. I started scraping the label away with my left thumbnail. Maybe there was some trace beneath. Come on, rules of space and time. Throw me a bone here.

Meghan padded down the stairs.

"What are you doing?"

I ignored her and continued scraping. I was Ahab, and the letters beneath this label my giant white whale. Finally the label worked itself free, but there was nothing else beneath. No blue plastic label, no white letters. Just the sticky underside of the label I'd just removed.

"Mickey?"

Except . . .

There. It was faint, but legible. The outlines of six letters in the grime, pressed against the cheap metal.

"Come here. Can you read those letters?"

She was in this far, why not humor me for just a few more seconds? Standing next to me, she leaned forward, squinting.

"What is this, a test? D-E-R . . . H . . . no wait, A."

"Keep going."

"A-C-E . . . Derace?"

She pronounced it to rhyme with "terrace." Growing up, I'd always pronounced it to rhyme with "the ace."

Either way, the letters were there. It hadn't been a dream. I wasn't hallucinating.

Meghan put her hand on my shoulder.

"Do you know that name?"

EVEN MEGHAN COULDN'T LAWYER-LOGIC her way out of that one.

Fact: Grandpop Henry worked at the same mental institution that housed the man who killed my father with a steak knife. I produced the paystubs, I showed Meghan the *Daily News* and *Bulletin* clips.

Fact: Grandpop Henry rented an apartment in the same building where the man who killed my father grew up.

Fact: Grandpop Henry kept a bottle of white pills locked up in his medicine cabinet that sent part of their user into the past.

"I'm not letting you have that one," Meghan said.

"Fine. Mysterious white pills that *allegedly* send the soul of their user back to the past. That okay, Counselor?"

"Conjecture. But fine, okay—let's say these pills do what you say. What was your grandfather planning to do?"

"Kill the man who killed his son. Change reality."

"Then why hasn't he done it? Think about it. If he's been taking these pills like you think he has, why isn't your life automatically different?"

"Maybe he tried. Maybe it's not as easy as it seems."

"Or maybe he tried it once and it sent him into his coma, because those pills are wildly dangerous."

I had been thinking the same thing. But I wasn't going to let her have the point that easily.

"Conjecture."

"Over-frickin'-ruled."

We stared at the each for a few minutes, letting our imaginations run wild. The whole idea was ludicrous, of course. But take the pills out of the equation. There were too many coincidences piled up. My grandpop had been trying something—revenge or closure.

"The only person who knows is my grandpop. And he can't talk. Not yet, anyway."

Meghan looked at me.

"He might not be the only one."

IX

ASYLUM ROAD

ONCE YOU WALK UP Oxford Avenue, away from the El, you enter Northwood, which has always been the nicest part of Frankford. In fact, if you lived in Northwood, you never admitted to living in Frankford.

Northwood had slightly wider streets—some of them brick-paved—with singles and twins and trees and big backyards and everything else everyone in Frankford wanted.

I grew up resenting the whole Frankford/Northwood divide. The dividing line, of course, was the Frankford El. We lived one block south of the El, in a cramped rowhome. Zero trees, a grim factory parking lot across the street.

But go just two blocks north of the El, and it's a completely different story. Aforementioned trees and backyards. Why couldn't my mom have moved there after my dad died? Just a few blocks away? Take a walk on the wild side, Anne. Sure, maybe the mortgage would have been a couple extra grand—maybe $11,000 as opposed to the $9,000 you'd pay in Frankford—but surely we could have swung that, right?

Couldn't we?

Mom had moved there eight years ago, finally leaving Darrah Street. I honestly don't know why she stayed in that house so long, other than inertia. I used to pretend that it was because she missed my father, that she couldn't bear the idea of moving away from the house they'd shared. But if that was true, she never let on. She almost never talked about him, and packed up every photo of him and put them in the hutch in the dining room. Maybe it was the lingering memory of my father, but I just think she hated the idea of moving.

So she'd traded a standard issue Frankford rowhome for the slightly more upscale standard Northwood twin. Instead of neighbors jammed up against both sides of her home, now she had a single neighbor jammed up against only one side of her home.

"MORE WINE, MEGHAN?"

"No thank you, Mrs. Wade."

"There's plenty here. And call me Anne, willya?"

"I'm okay. I have to drive later, and I really don't have much of a tolerance. I'm kind of a cheap date."

A mild lie from Meghan. She could hold her liquor like a bartop. She just didn't want to insult my mother's choice in grape-based libations. Not that she's a snob. But chances are, the Charles family never served pinot grigio from a cardboard box.

We all stood around the kitchen—me in my arm sling, Meghan, my mother and her boyfriend—making introductions and small talk. Mom was so stunned that I brought somebody, she didn't even notice the sling. In my twenty plus years of dating life, I've never brought anybody home. Ever.

But now I was happy for the witness, because Whiplash Walt was in rare form. Touching my mom's shoulders, her back, her waist— like he was planning on killing her later and wanted to place as many fingerprints as possible, just so the Philly PD would be extra-clear on who'd done it.

Whiplash Walt was a lawyer, just like Meghan's father, but they inhabited two totally different planes of existence. Nicholas Charles Esq. regularly lunched with the mayor and the Philadelphia political elite. Whiplash Walt spent his days handing out cards to anybody wearing a puffy neck brace within a five-mile radius. Whiplash, as his name might imply, did personal injury. It was how he'd met my mom, in fact. She tried to sue the hospital where she'd worked as an accountant for a slip-and-fall thing. She'd lost the case, but won Whiplash.

Mom asked me if I wanted another beer, but instead I helped myself to some of Whiplash's whiskey—Johnnie Walker Black. Probably a gift from a grateful client. God knows the cheap bastard wouldn't spring for it himself.

Mom excused herself to go to the basement. I knew where she was going.

"It's okay. It's your house. You can smoke here."

"You know I don't smoke, Mickey."

"I totally know you do."

"You're being silly."

I turned to Meghan.

"She totally smokes."

"I *do not* smoke."

Mom excused herself anyway to go downstairs to smoke. In a few moments we would hear the wrinkling of the wrapper, then the flick of the lighter. And in a few minutes we would all smell cigarette smoke.

I explained to Meghan, not bothering to lower my voice.

"Both of my mom's parents died of lung cancer. She wants me to think that she quit smoking in 1990, when her father died. And I really do think she tries to quit. She just never has."

Whiplash was clearly uncomfortable with this, so he made some small talk with Meghan. Once he found out her father was *the* Nicholas Charles, the small talk became more pointed, asking what her father was working on now, and hey, does he go to the Capital Grille every so often, and hey, is your dad looking to hire oh I'm just kidding but really I'm not.

My mom returned to the kitchen, absolutely reeking of smoke. It wafted from her clothes and invaded our nostrils. I fought back the urge to sneeze. We all sat down to eat.

Within sixty seconds Whiplash had whipped through his dinner. Then he stood up and wordlessly made his way down to his basement office. But not before giving my mom a none-too-subtle pinch on her ass.

The plates in front of Meghan and me were still full, as we hadn't had time to pretend to enjoy more than a few bites of our rigatoni and meatballs. My mom leaned in closer to us, all confidential-like.

"He's working on a case."

I leaned in, too.

"Don't worry about it."

Whiplash spent a lot of time in Northwood, but he'd never move here. Going from suburbia to Northwood would be serious slumming, even for a personal injury lawyer. So he kept his own condo in Ardmore, but spent most of his time at my mom's house.

"More wine?"

"I'm good, Mrs. Wade."

"Hey, I told you. It's Anne. We're all adults here."

"Right. Anne."

Bringing Meghan had been a tactical decision. With a buffer in the room, my mom might not come at me with both barrels blazing. She might even be forced to answer a question or two directly.

"Mom, what do you know about Grandpop and the Adams Institute?"

The fork in my mother's hand froze for a brief moment, like the fancy slow-mo bullet time of a Wachowski flick. She smiled.

"That's where I thought I'd end up when you told me you wanted to be a writer."

And then the fork completed the journey to her mouth, which chewed and grinned at the same time.

The Adams Institute was a popular punch line in Frankford. Misbehave, and your parents would say, "You're going to drive me straight to Adams if you don't knock that off." Or, "Where we going on vacation, Mom?" "To Adams, if you don't stop goofing around." Adams was the loony bin. It was the most beautiful piece of land in Frankford, spread across ten gorgeous acres on the fringes of Northwood. But nobody wanted to end up there.

Meghan laughed politely.

"How many years did Mickey's grandfather work there?"

Oooh, *kapowie*. Anne hadn't seen that one coming. She was very practiced at smacking away my questions. She had since I was a kid. But the two-on-one assault had left her flummoxed.

"Oh, gee. I think he retired a few years ago? We really don't talk too much. You know your grandpop, Mickey."

I took a slug of Johnny Walker Black for courage.

"How long before Grandpop found out Billy Derace was there?"

You should have seen the death stare on Anne's face then. My God. Blue eyes like dagger icicles.

"Billy who?"

"*Mom.* The guy who killed dad."

"Excuse me."

My mom pushed her chair back, wiped her mouth with a white napkin, placed it on the table, then left the room.

Meghan and I exchanged glances. I took another gulp of Whiplash's good scotch, which burned my throat as I followed my mom into the kitchen.

MY MOTHER'S PALMS WERE pressed to the edges of the countertop. I didn't know if she was trying to keep her balance or keep the counter from resisting the earth's gravity and floating into the air.

"Mom?"

She looked up. Tears were running down her cheeks. I had the strangest sense of déjà vu. Wasn't I just here—my mother looking at me and crying? Like, thirty-seven years ago?

My mom wiped her face dry.

"You don't understand. For years I've been waiting for the call that your grandfather's murdered someone over at Adams."

"Not just someone. *Billy Derace.* Why didn't you ever tell me the truth? You said it was a bar fight. But this guy just attacked Dad out of nowhere. I read the news clips."

"When would you have liked to know? When you were nine years old? Or maybe when you turned sixteen? Twenty-one, just in time for you to go out drinking?"

"Any of those times would have been better than you lying to me."

"I never lied to you. You assumed things."

This was true. I had filled in the gaps. But only because I'd never heard the full story, and had little else to go on. My mother was masterful at shutting down awkward conversations or ignoring them completely.

I tried a different way at it.

"I found a bunch of newspaper clippings that Grandpop kept—all about Dad's murder. I think he saved every newspaper article, and even got a copy of the police report."

"Well, that's a surprise. Your father hated your grandfather and always assumed the feeling was mutual. Who knew he gave a shit."

It was always that. Your grandfather. Your side of the family. Your gene pool, not mine.

"Why did he hate Grandpop?"

"It's a long story, and we have a guest."

Now it was "we." Now I was part of the family again. Our weird dysfunctional family of two.

"Okay, now here's what I don't get. You don't like him. That much is obvious. You never speak to him, you barely seem to tolerate his existence, and yet you're always bugging me to visit him. You put me in his friggin' apartment, Mom. Why would you push me toward somebody you hate? Somebody you tell me my own father hated?"

"Because he doesn't have anybody else."

"That doesn't make any sense."

"And because someday he might wake up. And the doctors say if he does wake up, he's going to need some help. I can't do it, not with work. You're his grandson."

Then I understood what my mom had wanted all along. A way to ease her conscience. A way to take care of everything. Me. And my grandpop.

That is: me taking care of my grandpop. Because she sure as hell didn't want to deal with him.

We didn't say anything for a short while. I knew Meghan could hear every word of this. My mother's house, as spacious as it may be by Northwood standards, wasn't a Main Line McMansion.

"Why did Dad hate Grandpop? Was it because of the divorce?"

"I should have never brought that up."

"Come on, what's the difference now? Dad's gone, and Grandpop is not in a position to care."

"I wish you'd just forget about it."

"No, I'm not going to forget about it. This is bullshit. Can you for once, please, just tell me something about my family so I don't have to keep on inventing details?"

Oh, the look my mother gave me. A withering, icy-blue stare that instantly reduced me to a child.

"I didn't find this out until after you were born, but apparently your grandfather used to beat up your grandmother."

My skin went cold as I imagined my grandmother—my sweet grandmother who had nothing but kind words and cookies for me growing up—being struck.

Mom saw she had me. She kept going.

"Your father said he really didn't remember it until after you were born. But when he became a parent, I guess it all came flooding back. He was depressed all the time, and spent most family holidays avoiding your grandpop Henry—only talking to him when he had to. And that's the way their relationship stayed until your father died. Now can we finish dinner?"

IN 1917 A PHILADELPHIA developer named Gustav Weber went to Los Angeles on his honeymoon. He fell so deeply and promptly in love with the Spanish mission-style architecture that he decided to re-create a piece of Southern California on the East Coast. Upon his return, Weber bought a triangle of land on the outskirts of Philadelphia, divided it up into blocks with street names like Los Angeles Avenue and San Gabriel Road, and then built the homes of his dream: stucco bungalows with red-tiled roofs.

Weber, however, didn't take into account the harsh East Coast winters that killed the plants and froze the occupants of the uninsulated homes. By the time the Great Depression hit, Weber was bankrupt.

But Hollywood never died.

My grandmom had lived there—at 603 Los Angeles Avenue, near San Diego Avenue—ever since I can remember. While her ex hopped around various apartments in Frankford over the years, Ellie Wadcheck—she never went back to her maiden name— stayed put. I used to waste away many summer afternoons in the postage stamp–sized yard behind her house. Especially in the years after my father died, and my mom needed someone to watch me.

I didn't think anything was weird about Hollywood, PA, until I went to college, and discovered that my friends thought I was full of crap.

Meghan didn't believe me either—at first.

"She lives where?"

"Hollywood. It's a neighborhood in Abington."

"How have I never heard of this?"

"Oh oh oh, you're a rich girl, and you've gone too far . . ."

"Shut up."

We stopped at the Hollywood Tavern. I didn't have a chance to finish my Johnnie Walker Black at my mother's, and I needed another drink. Meghan decided she could use one, too. Maybe something that didn't come from a box.

The place was a former show home for the Weber development that was later fitted with a brick addition that stuck out like a cancerous growth on the face of the mission-style pad. Inside, the bar was designed for serious drinking and sports watching. I ordered a Yuengling; Meghan had a white wine.

"My God, you weren't full of crap. This place looks like it was scraped out of the Hollywood Hills, flung across the country and it landed here."

"Pretty amazing, isn't it?"

"Did any famous actors grow up here?"

"I don't think so. Unless you consider Joey Lawrence famous."

We drank. I pretended to watch baseball—a Phillies night game. But mostly I was thinking about what my mother had said.

GRANDMOM ELLIE WAS SURPRISED to see me. I never dropped by unannounced. In fact, I usually tried to wriggle out of family commitments whenever I could. Not that I didn't like to see my family, but I always found the first ten to twenty minutes of reacclamation to be awkward and painful. There was always an undercurrent of guilt to it—*gee, it's been so long, Mickey, you're never around, you don't seem to want to associate with the rest of us . . . but anyway, how are things? How's the writing career coming along?*

But Meghan took the edge off. Oh, how my grandmom fawned over her.

"Look at how beautiful you are! My God. Mickey, do you tell this beautiful woman how gorgeous she is every day?"

"Hi, Mrs. Wadcheck. So great to meet you."

Meghan even pronounced the name like a pro. She was a quick study, that one.

"Oh, you're so lovely."

The interior of my grandmom's bungalow hadn't changed . . . ever. If I were to pop one of those white pills now, I have a feeling I wouldn't be able to tell the difference between the early 1970s and now until I stepped outside and checked the cars. Everything was off-white or blinding yellow. Yellow is her favorite color.

Grandmom insisted on serving us giant tumblers of Frank's

vanilla cream soda—which let me tell you, does not go well with Yuengling or Johnnie Walker Black—as well as a tray of the most sickeningly sweet butter ring cookies I've ever tasted. If she noticed that I only picked up my soda with three fingers of my left hand, she didn't let on.

Instead, Ellie Wadcheck smiled at us, but you could tell she was waiting for the other shoe to drop. You could count the times I'd dropped by just to visit on . . . my missing right arm.

"I wanted to ask you about something, Grandmom."

Deep in the throes of sugar shock, I lied and said I was writing a piece about my father, and how he'd died. In my defense, I wasn't totally lying. Maybe there was a magazine piece in this, or even a book. But writing about my father and his killer hadn't yet occurred to me. It was just something to say to my grandmom.

She smiled at us.

"Billy Derace was the son of a whore."

Meghan and I sat there, momentarily stunned.

"Don't hold back, Grandmom. Tell us how you really feel."

Grandmom laughed. She was pretty much the only relative who thought I was remotely funny.

"Oh, I didn't know her. But she was notorious. I'll never forgive that Billy Derace for what he did, but I'm not surprised, considering how he was raised. He was born to a very immature mother. She married young, but refused to stay home. She worked all day and went out drinking and dancing every night. Eventually the husband had enough, he left. Everyone in the neighborhood talked about it."

"This was Frankford?"

"Yes—where I lived with your grandfather until I moved here. Anyway, there was a rumor that Billy had a younger brother who died when he was young—only three years old, they say. And Billy was the one watching him when he died."

Meghan turned pale.

"What happened?"

"The story goes that he choked on a piece of cereal. Billy didn't know what to do. This was . . . oh, 1968? 1969? Nobody taught children the Heimlich maneuver back then."

"Where was his mother? In 1969, Billy had to be only nine or ten years old."

"Yes, he was. His mother was out at a bar, and I suppose she thought that a nine-year-old was mature enough to care for a toddler. Billy and his brother were often left to fend for themselves."

Meghan glanced over at me, eyebrow raised a little—but I was already taking mental notes. A three-year-old choking to death would certainly have made the newspapers back in the late 1960s, wouldn't it? But then why wasn't Billy taken from his irresponsible mother?

"So Billy was probably a little crazy."

My grandmom paused.

"Well, he wasn't a normal child."

"And he probably grew up crazy, and then one day in 1980 attacked my father with a steak knife at random."

Grandmom looked at me.

"I don't think it was random."

THROUGHOUT HIS SHORT LIFE, Anthony Wade never made much money. Some other dads, it seemed—the fathers of kids I knew in college—couldn't help but walk out onto their front lawns and find $100 bills sticking to the bottoms of their shoes. Some fathers inherited their money; others chose careers that more or less guaranteed them a lot of money; still others worked very hard and eventually made a lot of money.

My father worked hard, but never made much money.

The Wadcheck men seemed to be drawn to the two professions that sound cool but suck ass when it comes to making money: writing and music. Unless you're lucky. And if you're lucky, you don't need writing or music. You just need to be lucky, as well as the ability to open up your wallet as the greenbacks come tumbling from the skies.

My father gigged with his band or solo almost every weekend of my childhood, but the most he made was $100 at a time—and that was for two nights of performing, five hours each night. And that was in the late 1970s, early 1980s. When I was born, my mom told me, he'd be lucky to come home with $25 in his pocket.

And a lot of that money usually went to musical equipment—replacing guitar strings, saving up for new speakers or effects pedals.

My father was perfectly content with the amount of money he made playing music. His art supported his art.

What it didn't do was support his young wife and infant son.

So Anthony Wade had to work at least two other jobs at all times—usually steady but grinding custodial work for whoever was hiring in Frankford at the moment. He also gave guitar lessons to whoever could cough up $5 for a half hour of instruction.

Even when I was a kid I knew my father was miserable with these other jobs. His mood determined the mood of the house. And many weekdays, his mood was lousy.

This probably explained why, when I embarked upon my own low-paying career as a journalist, I avoided the pitfall of a wife and kids. If my profession supported my profession, then that was C is for Cookie, good enough for me. At least I wasn't dragging anyone down with me.

But I didn't know the half of it. Because my grandmom started to explain that layoffs were so common, and money so thin, my dad would take other kinds of jobs. Jobs that, she said, broke her heart.

"Your father let them do all kinds of tests on him."

"Who?"

"Those people at the institute. You know, the one up the boulevard."

The ex-journalist in me started feeling the tingles. Stories were all about connections. Here was another connection with that lunatic asylum.

"You mean the Adams Institute? What kind of tests?"

Grandmom frowned as if she'd swallowed a fistful of lemon seeds.

"Government drug tests. This was around the time you were born. He'd signed up after reading an ad in the newspaper. Young, fit, healthy male subjects needed for government pharmaceutical studies. Two hundred a week, guaranteed for four to six weeks."

"I thought the Adams Institute was a mental hospital."

"Most of it is, but they also did tests. Oh, Mickey, you should have seen him. My twenty-three-year-old son suddenly looked like he was forty years old, bags under his eyes, yellow skin—he looked like he hadn't slept in a week."

The image of my father in my mind was of a man much older than his physical years. I remember being stunned when I hit my early thirties, and realized that I had just outlived my father. I didn't look like I'd gone skinny dipping in the fountain of youth, but I also didn't look as old as the father in my memory.

Meghan reached out and touched Grandmom's hand.

"You never found out what kinds of drugs he was given?"

"Blind tests, Anthony told me. They didn't tell him what they were pumping into his veins—they only promised there'd be no long-lasting side effects. I think that was nonsense. Your father was never the same after those tests."

And I had a feeling I knew who'd been administering those tests.

"NO."

"Come on."

"No. The last time you took these pills, you woke up and wouldn't talk to me. The time before that, you lost feeling in your right arm. Are we sensing a pattern here, Mickey?"

"How else am I supposed to figure out what really happened? I have to ask Erna Derace. Ask her everything she knows about Mitchell DeMeo and his tests."

After the weird dinner with my mother and the visit to Grand-mom in Hollywood, Meghan had driven me back to Frankford Avenue. I assumed she'd be heading on her way, but she followed me up and then kneeled down and started picking through the boxes and crates again. I asked her what she was looking for, and she gave me a *duh* look that I probably deserved. Meghan was looking for DeMeo's notes, of course. Anything to do with Billy Derace, or my father. Preferably both. Something that would explain the random attack in Brady's that night.

But I had had another idea. A shortcut.

Asking Billy's mom.

"Such a bad idea," Meghan said.

"How else am I supposed to figure this out?"

"Gee, I don't know, how about the old-fashioned way—*research*. You were a reporter, right? I mean, you weren't pulling one long scam on me or something, thinking I had a thing for press cards and long skinny notebooks?"

"Did you?"

"Alas, you're not a reporter anymore."

"I still have a few long skinny notebooks."

We spent some more time poring through the dusty cardboard boxes full of notes and newspaper clippings and files that didn't make any sense. Meghan found a motherlode of family trees, but no "Deraces" or "Wadchecks." No notes that would explain the "tests" my dad was given.

Around nine Meghan asked if I had anything to eat around the apartment. I asked her if she liked peanut butter and apples.

"Let's order something that is not peanut- or apple-related. My treat."

"You forgot the beer. Grains are an important part of the Alex Alonso diet."

We ended up calling for pizza from a place down the street. I walked under the El to pick it up, and burned my three good fingers on the box carrying it back. A guy in a tattered gray sweater asked me for a slice. I told him sorry, I was just delivering it. He told me to go screw myself. I love this neighborhood.

By the time I carried the pizza two flights up, though, I had convinced myself that the pills were the way to go. Meghan disagreed.

"Those pills are going to fry your brain. Do you want to end up in a coma like your grandfather?"

"I'm not eighty-four years old. And besides, you told me they were placebos. Sugar pills."

"My friend doesn't know everything. In fact, I seem to remember that he almost flunked biochemistry sophomore year."

"Look, I don't have a choice. I need to figure out the connection between Billy Derace and my father. Maybe I can push it and go to the late 1970s, or even 1980. I can snoop around and see what I can piece together."

"You told me you tried and you couldn't go any further than 1975."

Meghan blinked, caught herself, turned to the side.

"Okay, for the record, I can't believe I made a statement like that . . ."

"Look, maybe I didn't try hard enough. Maybe it's not just supposed to come to you."

"Hmmm."

From there we ate our slices in silence. It was ghetto pizza. Very thin on the sauce, with bad, greasy cheese. Frankford didn't have much going for it in the 1970s, but it once had the be-all, end-all of Philadelphia foods: slices of Leandro's Pizza. The tiny shop used to be on the ground floor of the stairwell leading up to the El stop. Step off the El, you couldn't help but follow that intoxicating scent all the way down the concrete staircases, and the next thing you knew your hand was stuffed in your pants pocket, fingertips searching for the two quarters, one dime and one nickel it would cost to procure a slice. During my jaunts to the past I'd purposefully avoided Leandro's. It would be like a eunuch visiting the Playboy Mansion.

By midnight we'd turned up very little that made any sense—so many of the notes and clips were about Philadelphians who were living in the 1920s and 1930s, none of them Deraces or Wadchecks.

So I finally convinced Meghan that the white pills were the way to go. Wearily, she agreed.

And then I remembered that I'd locked them in the medicine cabinet.

"LET ME GUESS. YOU have no idea where the key is."

"Nope."

"Do you have a hammer?"

"I don't know. You snooped around here all night. Did you see a hammer?"

"What's in the silverware drawer?"

"I have silverware?"

Meghan checked the wooden slide-out drawer that contained a number of puzzling kitchen tools—none of them a hammer. Corkscrews. Many rusted beer bottle openers, some of them emblazoned with the logos of long-dead Philly brews like Schmidt's and Ortlieb's. There was a large, plastic-handled steak knife, but it didn't look like the type that could saw through a tin can, let alone a padlock.

"I think I saw a dustpan and whisk broom in the closet. Would you mind double-checking that?"

"What, are you going to sweep the lock away?"

"No. I'm going to use something big and heavy—your head comes to mind—and shatter your medicine cabinet. Again, for the record, I can't believe I'm saying these particular words out loud."

"Why don't you let me smash it?"

"You've got three good fingers. Do you really want to lose another one or two?"

She wrapped her right hand in a dirty gray oven mitt that looked like it had been used to hand-stomp out a grease fire, then picked up a heavy glass ashtray. She walked into the bathroom and a second later, I heard a loud pop and shatter. Then nothing.

"Are you okay?"

"Well, it's open."

I looked inside. The door was obliterated, glimmering fragments of mirror were all over the sink, floor, toilet seat and tub.

"I thought you were going to, like, do it on the count of three or something."

"Would that have made you feel better?"

We cleaned up the glass and I plopped myself down on the couch. Meghan sat on the floor next to me, on her knees.

"What are you doing?"

"I thought maybe I could still talk to you when you were . . . you know, back in the past. I heard you mumbling in your sleep. Maybe you're still connected with this time when you go on your little trips."

"Am I supposed to be able to hear you?"

"I'll shout. Come on, this is your idea. I'm just trying to help."

I took two pills, looking into Meghan's pretty eyes. She reached out to hold my hand. My eyelids grew heavy, slammed shut. When I woke up on February 28, 1972, I was looking at Erna Derace.

She was holding a gun.

X

SLASHER'S REVENGE

ERNA DERACE WAS SITTING on the backs of her heels, the polka-dot dress fanned around her. The gun was a small, pearl-handled .38 revolver. I was fairly confident it was the same gun Dr. DeMeo held in his meaty paw and waved around my ghostly face a few days ago. Apparently, she'd taken it from his desk drawer. I could tell because the drawer was still open. And inside were papers and files, stuffed in horizontally.

She held the .38 casually, like it was a TV remote, and she'd become so absorbed in a show that she'd forgotten it was in her hand.

"Dammit . . . not again."

She spoke softly, staring at the floor.

Was she about to kill herself? Or DeMeo? I tried to calm her down, even though I was invisible.

"I know you can't hear or see me. But if there's any way my words can find their way into your brain, please hear me now—I really think it would be a good idea to put down that gun."

"I can hear you."

I froze in place.

"What?"

She turned and locked eyes with me.

"I can see you, too. I can see *all of you*. I've been pretending I can't because I know you're probably just a figment of my imagination. I thought if I stopped paying attention maybe you'd go away. But you never go away. None of you do."

"You saw me in the room that first night? When you were with DeMeo?"

"Yes. I was hoping you'd go away if I went down on him. You did."

"What exactly do you think I am?"

"You're a dead man."

"But I'm not."

"Right. Sure. You're not dead. Maybe I'm dead. Maybe I'm a dead woman floating around a sea of living people, only I don't know it yet. Maybe I've been dead since I was a kid."

"I want to ask you about DeMeo."

"He's good to me."

"What does he do up here? What kinds of experiments?"

"You mean you don't know? I thought dead people knew everything. That's why you come back. To taunt the living. To show us how smart you are, and how dumb the rest of us are."

"Well, I *don't* know. You can lord it over me."

"I don't know either. Mitchell says it's top secret. All I know is that his patients arrive after dark, and they stay for sometimes an hour, sometimes all night. He says he works better in the dark, so he keeps the windows covered, and he unscrewed the lamps in the hallway. I'm allowed to have light in my apartment, but no-where else. And he likes it quiet. It must be absolutely quiet at all times."

I thought of Billy Derace, sitting in the one lit room in an otherwise dark apartment building. A twelve-year-old, being forced to stay inside and be quiet.

"I see your son sometimes, sitting outside of your apartment. Sometimes he's crying. Sometimes he's *bleeding*, Erna."

"What are you saying?"

"You know what I'm saying."

"You don't understand what it's like."

"Try me."

"No, I'd rather not. You're going to disappear soon, too. Maybe you'll leave me alone, maybe you'll do something rude to me, but either way I'm never going to see you again. Just like the others. No guy wants a kid around that's not his. Even Dr. DeMeo doesn't like that he's around. He always tells me to keep him quiet, he can't concentrate on his work. And that little son of a bitch just doesn't listen. He's just like his father . . ."

"Your son needs you."

More important, I need you to be there for your son.

She gestured at me with the gun as she spoke.

"No. It's too late. There's too much of Victor in him. He fights me on everything, no matter what I say. No matter how hard I work for him. You try talking to him. Easy for you to sit there and say *your son needs you.* You have no idea."

"Who's Victor?"

"My ex, Victor D'Arrazzio. The kid's father. That why I pulled this out. I thought I saw him yesterday."

"What, so you want to shoot him? You should put that back in the drawer. Take a deep breath. Go downstairs and lay down."

"No, I don't think I will. I'm either going to put a bullet in my head or I'm going to go out drinking. It's the only thing that keeps the likes of you away. All of you dead people. So I'll either ignore you or join you."

"What dead people? I'm not dead, Erna. It's complicated, but I assure you, I'm not dead."

"Prove it."

She leaned in closer. I could smell her perfume, sweet and pungent. Her lips opened slightly. She moved closer still.

"What are you doing?"

Before she could answer our lips collided. I felt her hand touching mine, our fingers interlocking. She squeezed mine.

Soon nothing made physical sense. We were in the room, we were all over the room, we were inside each other's skin. I had no sense of where my lips or my fingers ended. No sense of where I stopped and this woman began.

Without warning, she broke our embrace, looked up at me. I pushed away.

"You think I'm dead, and you kiss me?"

"I wanted to know what death tastes like. It tastes *good*."

Outside the El train cars rumbled down their tracks, vibrating the floorboards beneath our feet.

"Please put the gun away."

"Why? What do you have to be nervous about? You're already dead. Even if I aimed this gun straight at your head and pulled the trigger the bullet would sail right through you."

I had nothing to say to that, mostly because I worried she *was* going to swing the revolver over at me and squeeze the trigger, just to test her theory. I had no idea if the bullets would sail through my head or not. I didn't want to find out.

And then the pill wore off.

WHEN I WOKE UP in the present Meghan was sitting on the floor, pen in her hand and legal pad on her lap. She wasn't writing anything. She hadn't written anything.

She didn't say anything.

I sat up, rubbed my eyes.

"You're not going to believe what just happened."

She stood up and walked across the room. She turned and half-sat on the cherrywood desk, then finally looked at me.

"Meghan?"

"I can't believe you actually kissed that woman."

"Oh. I'm guessing you heard all of that."

"Your end of the conversation. But don't change the subject, Mickey. You were making out with the mother of the guy who killed your father."

"It wasn't my idea."

"What?"

"I was unconscious and nearly four decades in the past. It just kind of happened."

"So what—were you hoping to heal your girlfriend Erna there with the magical power of your lips? Do you realize, Mickey, that if that woman's still alive, she's like sixty or seventy by now?"

"She said she saw other dead people. What does that mean? That other people like me are traveling back in time?"

She looked at me, again at a loss for words. This wasn't like Meghan at all. She was the perfect friend because she had this warm, relaxed way of filling the uncomfortable spaces. Usually, I loved to listen to her talk. But not now.

"What, Meghan, what? What's wrong?"

"There's something else."

"What."

"While you were . . . under, asleep, whatever . . . you uh . . ."

"Spit it out."

"You ejaculated."

"I *what*? Are you sure?"

"I'm a big girl, Mickey. I've seen it happen from time to time. But not like it happened with you. You looked like you were either having a seizure or an orgasm."

"Oh God."

"You didn't try to swallow your tongue, so my guess was orgasm."

"Oh God."

Meghan looked at me, uneasy smile on her face. "Quit it with the Oh Gods, or I'll think you're doing it again."

"I'm sorry. Oh God."

"So let me ask you again: What were you doing with the mother of your father's killer?"

This was too much. She'd kissed me, she'd merged with me—or whatever the hell had happened. I didn't remember it being necessarily sexual. I remember it being extremely disorienting.

Finally I stood up and went to the bathroom and cleaned myself up with the three fingers I had left. Meghan hadn't been lying.

When I returned to the main room we seemed to have this unspoken agreement not to speak about whatever had just happened. Maybe it was a side effect of the pill. Hell, maybe they weren't time-traveling pills after all. Maybe Grandpop Henry had a secret stash of Cialis in that Tylenol bottle and I was a sick bastard imagining this whole thing.

But I knew that wasn't the case. Meghan knew it, too.

"So to recap, we're out of witnesses. Your mother doesn't know anything. Your grandmother gave us a little. And Erna can do wonders with her lips."

Meghan was wrong. We had another witness.

"There's someone else."

"Who?"

"Billy Derace."

SOMETIME IN THE MIDDLE of the night I woke up. I listened to Meghan's breathing for a while, then realized she was awake, too. I reached out and touched her hand lightly.

"You awake?"

"Yeah. You?"

"Yeah."

We lay there in the dark together. I was genuinely surprised when she suggested crashing again. She told me it was late, she didn't feel like making the drive back downtown this time of night—making it not a big deal. But still: she stayed. She didn't have to. Even my pill-popping wet dream hadn't scared her away. Even me, making out with a woman who was probably seventy years old by now. It made me wonder. Finally, I asked her.

"Why are you doing all of this?"

"All of what?"

"You know. Everything. Helping me trying to figure this out. Hanging out so much. Not calling the lunatic asylum to have me carted away."

She was silent for a moment.

"You want the truth?"

"Of course."

"Don't get me wrong—you're a great guy, and I cherish our friendship."

"Uh-huh."

"And I was really concerned when I thought you were slipping into some kind of *Trainspotting*-style drug oblivion—I mean, I couldn't just stand on the sidelines and do nothing, you know? But now I know there's something else going on, and the more I hear, the more I'm curious, and . . . well, I don't mean to sound cold or anything, but I really just want to know how it all turns out."

Somehow it was honest and warm and heartbreaking at the same time.

WE SLEPT MOST OF the next day away. The rain was pelting down when we pulled up to the Adams Institute in the early evening. There was a frightening rumble in the distance. It was one of those good down-and-dirty early summer storms you get every so often in Philadelphia.

"And here we are, sneaking into a mental hospital," Meghan said.

"We're not sneaking in. We're just going to walk."

"Easy for you to say. You must have done this all the time at the *City Press*. Smooth-talking your way past security, slipping through unlocked doors . . ."

"Uh, not exactly."

"You didn't sneak into government buildings? Secretly tape meetings? Spend endless nights taping together shredded documents?"

"There were reporters who loved that kind of thing. But I wasn't one of those reporters. I preferred the phone—or even better, an e-mail exchange. To tell you the truth, I even hated that—it always felt like I was bothering people."

"You're a regular Bob Woodward."

"I'm not even a Carl Bernstein. Lock me in a room with piles of documents and I'm a happy man."

"You live in a room with piles of documents, and you're miserable."

"Oh shut up."

All I wanted was thirty seconds with Billy Derace. That's all. If he recognized me, then it was proof that all of this was real, that I was speaking to him in the past. That I was the kindly ghost from upstairs who tried to stop his mother from beating him. Of course, I was also the kindly ghost who'd kissed his mother. But I wouldn't bring that up.

The front gate was just off Roosevelt Boulevard. Even the tall, black, wrought-iron fence surrounding the neatly manicured estate seemed to hold up a hand and say AND JUST WHERE DO YOU THINK YOU'RE GOING.

The plan was this: Meghan would pretend to be a lawyer from a nonexistent firm (she'd even printed up fake letterhead) with documents for an inmate (William Allen Derace) about an estate matter. Meghan was attractive, confident and knew how to lay down some lawyerspeak after years of watching her father.

The front receptionist desk shot her down completely. Meghan was told that the lead attorney would have to call to make an appointment.

She came back out to the car, sat down in the driver's seat, dripping wet. She fumed so hard, I swear I saw raindrops on her forehead sizzle and evaporate into steam. Meghan was not used to being shut out of anything.

I had no choice but to say:

"Okay, let me try."

She looked at me.

"I thought you didn't do this kind of thing."

"I'm thinking it'll look good on my résumé."

I was wearing my one jacket and a pair of ill-fitting trousers from my grandfather's closet, as well as one of his dress shirts. We had been roughly the same size at some point, but the man had shrunk in his old age, leaving everything a little tight. If only I had a skinny tie, I could join a new wave power pop boy band.

"Let me borrow your clipboard."

"Why?" Meghan asked.

"If you wear the right suit and carry a clipboard, you can pretty much walk into any building and nobody will bother you."

"Is that the right suit?"

"I'll walk fast so they don't notice."

I reached over with my three good fingers and started to pull on the door handle.

"Wish me luck."

"Good luck. By the way, if you're caught by the guards, wet your pants and start barking like a dog."

"You think this is a riot, don't you."

"No, I'm serious. That's the one thing that can get you out of pretty much any situation. Or at least, give you a chance to make a break for it."

"I'll be back as soon as I can."

The front lawn of the Adams Institute was manicured to within an inch of its life, and glistening with the humid rain. I strode forward purposefully, unapologetically. I was faking it like you wouldn't believe.

Inside the main hall there was a reception desk. I blew right past it and continued down a marble-floored hallway. Someone said "hey!" but I turned a corner, looking for a wall-mounted directory. There was a door to my right, then another set of stairs, then another door . . . which took me outside again, into the rain. Crap.

Not knowing exactly where to go, I darted down the side of the building, feeling the water creep down my collar, until I found a path that led into a group of trees. There were more buildings, two and four stories each, dotting the grounds. Derace could be in any one of them. Or not here at all.

I kept strolling, not too fast to be obvious. By the time I reached the tree line I could see another building off to the left—a 1950s-style, no-nonsense two-story deal. Which one of these things is not like the other? If I were going to run government drug experiments, would I do it in one of the storied old buildings that had been around since the Civil War, or would I use federal money to slap up something new? The name on the building said: THE PA-PIRO CENTER.

And that was as far as I got before I felt a hand on my good arm.

I HALF-EXPECTED A GUARD, but instead it was a man in a white robe and slippers. Late fifties, with brown hair combed straight back. His eyes were the most intense I'd ever seen. They practically glowed.

"I remember you," he said. "I met you when you were a kid. On that boat. Do you remember?"

I had no idea who he was, or what boat he was talking about.

"You and your sister. You were lost. On that boat."

See, right there were strikes one and two. I was an only child, and I grew up a landlubber. Mom didn't bring us on any yachts or cruise ships. She didn't even bring us to the *Good Ship Lollypop* down at Penn's Landing, like every other kid I knew.

"Sorry," I told the guy. "I don't remember."

He leaned forward and winked at me.

"My name is Dean. But that's just an alias."

Dean looked around to see if anyone else was listening. I looked around, too, to see if any armed guards were running toward us. But we were alone. Unfortunately.

Sometimes, though, a reporter can't be picky about his sources. It was a long shot, but I looked at Dean.

"Do you know a man here named William Derace? Billy Allen Derace?"

Dean's eyes widened.

"Of course I know that bastard. You should stay away from him—he's incredibly dangerous. I've been trying to collect him for years, but they keep him locked up all the time. Oh, the murders I could solve with that son of a bitch locked in my skull."

Okay, this guy was probably loony tunes, but it was also possible that he conflated actual reality with his fantasy life. Maybe he really did know Derace.

"Where do they keep him locked up?"

"No," Dean said. "Can't tell you that. Too dangerous. You don't want anything to do with Billy Derace. They keep that menace on sedatives twenty-four/seven. Weird shit happens when he wakes up."

"Come on, Dean. For old time's sake."

"You trying to con an old con? Nothing doing."

But Dean's eyes gave it away anyway. They flicked over to his right. Toward that 1950s building I'd spotted. The Papiro Center.

Dean tried cover it up by changing the topic.

"So how's your sister?"

"I don't have a sister. I'm an only child."

"Sure you do—the two of you were together on the *Moshulu*, when you got lost at the Bicentennial. You know, the little blond-haired girl eating the popcorn with you."

That stopped me cold. Suddenly I knew who he was talking about, but it wasn't my sister. It had been my mom's youngest sister, who was only nine months older than me.

We had been down at Penn's Landing because my father had been hired to play with a band called The Shuttlebums in front of

Winston's Restaurant. And across a pedestrian bridge was a huge clipper ship, since converted to a restaurant, called the *Moshulu*. During the summer of 1976 my dad was working maintenance on that boat.

Mid-gig, I somehow conned my aunt, who was all of five years old, into walking over the bridge and checking out the boat. My parents went insane with worry, but luckily we were picked up by an off-duty cop, who thought it was a little suspicious that two little kids sat themselves down at a small table meant for two—meaning, no room for parents.

"*You're* the guy who found us?" I asked. "How is that possible? How do you even recognize me?"

"It's not your face," he said. "It's your *soul*."

Okay then. I thanked him and then excused myself. Leave it to me to get lost as a kid, only to be found by a raving lunatic who could see other people's souls.

THE LIGHTS WERE MOSTLY out in the Papiro Center. The back doors were locked. The front door was locked and controlled by a keypad. Why did I think it would be open? This was a mental hospital.

I stood there, looking up at the building. I'd already trespassed; I'd feel like a moron just leaving without trying *something*.

Screw it.

I shouted.

"*BILLY DERACE!*"

This would either work right away, or not. If I saw a light on the ground floor, I'd bolt.

"*BILLY! DERACE!*"

Come on you nutcase. Get up out of bed, come to your window, look down. I'll know in a second if you recognize me. Which of these windows is yours?

Then, on the left side—movement. No light, just a shadow on shadows. Dark gray on black. A male figure? It was too hard to see.

Behind me I heard a cough. My head whipped around; nobody. I looked back up at the window.

Nothing.

Just the rain, smacking into the grass, the blacktop path leading back to the main building.

Suddenly security lights flickered to life all around me. Crap. The main office knew I was here. I ran back the way I came, figuring that I could slow down my hurried jog at the last minute and just stroll on out of there, clipboard in hand.

But the door I'd used to get out was locked, trapping me outside.

Trapping me on the grounds of a three-hundred-year-old insane asylum.

Okay, so I freaked out a little. I ran in the opposite direction, toward the fence near Adams Avenue, where we'd parked. At the very least, I thought I could yell to Meghan and let her know what happened before they tackled me to the wet grass and wrestled me into a straitjacket. Meghan's dad was a powerful lawyer. I'm sure he could get me out of this place. Eventually.

There were voices behind me. I ran faster. You never realize how much you depend on your arms for balance until you lose feeling in one of them. I felt like I was going to tip over at any minute. Which would make it much easier to wrestle me into a straitjacket.

As I approached the gate, I saw that Meghan was out of the car, waiting for me. Her hair was dripping wet, and she urged me forward with her hands.

"Hurry!"

I skidded to a halt and almost slammed into the gate.

"They've got me surrounded. Look, go call your dad and tell him you have a dumbass for a friend who thought it would be funny if he—"

"Give me your foot."

I looked down. Meghan was reaching through the bars, fingers intertwined, making a little step for me.

"No way. I'm too heavy. And I've only got one functioning arm."

"Will you just give me your foot? I'll push you over the fence."

I didn't have the chance to have a talk with my father about women; he died before I'd reached puberty. But even I knew that when a beautiful woman is standing in the pouring rain, offering to help lift you over the black metal fence outside an insane asylum, you take her up on the offer.

I stepped into Meghan's hands, then reached up for the top of the fence. I could tell immediately that she'd grossly underestimated my weight. Her hands felt like they were attached to rubber cables, ready to snap at any moment. I wanted to stop and apologize—*sorry I'm so heavy, Meghan. It's all of the beer I've been drinking.* But there wasn't time. Meghan summoned some kind of inner Incredible Hulk–style gamma ray strength and pulled her arms up, lifting me to where I could just grab the top of the gate with the three good fingers on my left hand.

I held on as tightly as I could, then swung my left foot up to the top of the fence. The rubber soles of my shoes clung to the metal for a fraction of a second, and it was enough time for Meghan to give me another superhuman push, and for me to pull myself up and over.

I was over the fence.

And then I was falling.

The good news was that I'd managed to not land on top of Meghan—she'd scurried out of the way the moment my foot left her hands. But as I landed, my right foot twisted. I had a fleeting moment of *wow, I actually managed to land on my feet* before I completely went down.

Meghan helped me up, asked if I could put any weight on it. I tried. I told her no. She told me to stop being a pansy, and then helped me limp back to her passenger seat. The water ran down through my hair and onto my face. I eased back into the seat, used my good hand to pull my bad leg into the car, then we took off, rocketing down Adams Avenue.

"Thank God you were by that fence."

I looked over at Meghan. Her hands were gripping the steering wheel tightly, and her arms were shaking. Probably from the exertion, the worry, the adrenaline.

She looked at me.

"I presume that was you, shouting the name 'Billy Derace'?"

"The doors were locked. What else could I do?"

She didn't respond. By the time we'd cleared about three blocks, there were no sirens, no pursing vehicles, no spotlights. We'd gotten away clean.

Which is what probably emboldened me to suggest something really stupid.

"Slow down and go back around."

"What are you talking about?"

"Go back and park on the other side of the grounds. I've got an idea."

"You can barely walk."

"I don't plan on walking."

. . .

I REACHED INTO MY overcoat pocket and pulled out a single white pill. I'd tucked one in there, just in case.

Meghan got it right away—there are no dull forks in her silverware drawer. Still, she thought it was a really stupid idea.

"What good is it for you to sneak into that place back in 1972? Billy Derace's only twelve years old, and he's living at home. He's not going to be placed here until years later."

"The Papiro Center is the place listed on DeMeo's letterhead. His office might be on Frankford Avenue, but he works out of this building, too. Maybe we couldn't find any notes about his experiments because he kept them all here."

"So you're just going to pass out on the front seat on my car. What am I supposed to say to the cops when they pull over to check out what I'm doing here? And you *know* they're going to pull over and check it out."

"Keep driving, then. Just don't go too far."

We used her car key to cut the pill in half. I figured that dosage should give me enough time to slip through the gates, through the front door and into that building.

At first I wasn't even sure it worked—the place looked exactly the same now as it did back in 1972. This was a well-maintained loony bin, and always had been. But then I realized I was sitting in the middle of the street on a cold dark night, and the cars around me were all vintage models. Meghan's Prius was nowhere to be seen.

I slipped right through the asylum gates—which weren't locked now. Guess security wasn't a big concern back in 1972.

There were sodium lights dotting the grounds, casting wide ovals of yellow light on the lawn. I stuck to the dark patches.

When I reached the front door I grit my teeth and closed my eyes and just went for it.

Then I was inside.

Past the reception area, the doctors' offices and up a narrow row of concrete stairs and into the main quarters . . .

Which were empty.

Nothing. Just gurneys, completely stripped of everything except their thin mattresses.

Wasn't this where the experiments were supposed to be happening right about now? Did I miss them? Did I have the wrong building, after all?

I spent time back downstairs in the offices, rooting through filing cabinets, but they were empty, too.

By the time I thought to slip across the grounds and try another building, I could feel the dizziness starting again, and my grip on everything slipping away.

I WOKE UP GROGGY. Throbbing. Taste of sour metal in my mouth. Sweat all over my face, and nostrils full of a gamey scent that I quickly realized was *me*.

Meghan was next to me, driving.

"Did you find anything?"

"No."

I INSISTED ON PARKING at the hospital garage again, even though it meant a five-block walk for me on a bad ankle. Climbing up to the third floor wasn't fun either. Meghan tried to hide it, but she couldn't keep the smile off her face as we slowly made our way up.

"I still can't believe you just shouted his name."

"Fine. Next time we break into a mental hospital, you go over the fence."

And then we reached my apartment door.

But it was already open.

WE COULD SEE THE torn-up wood where the burglar had used the crowbar. Probably took him less than five seconds—jam the steel into the wedge between door and frame, pull once, maybe twice, and presto, you're breaking and entering.

We immediately tried to figure out what was missing, but the place was so cluttered with boxes, it was difficult. I had no TV to steal, no fancy DVD players or jewelry.

Meghan walked over to the desk.

"Your laptop's still here."

"It's too ancient to pawn."

My father's albums were still stacked up against the Technics turntable, which was also a relief. The peanut butter and apples were still on the kitchenette counter. My books were still stacked up on the cherrywood desk.

"Wow. I think someone busted into your place, saw that you had jack shit, then turned around and left."

"I'm glad you think this is funny."

"I don't. Not really."

"I don't know whether I should be relieved or depressed."

I limped into the bathroom to wash my face, then used a hand towel to dry my hair a little, which was dripping from the storm. Since the medicine cabinet mirror was still smashed, I had no idea how I looked. When my hair's wet a certain way, you can see the top of my head where I'm starting to go bald. I usually try to comb it to cover it up. Now I knew why men preferred fedoras back in the day.

Hanging the towel up I could feel my ankle really starting to throb. An aspirin would probably help, but then I remembered that I didn't have any real aspirin; just the transport-you-back-in-time variety. Tylenol A.D. Take two and call me thirty years ago.

Wait.

"Meghan!"

"What?"

"Did you move the bottle of pills?"

She appeared in the doorway.

"*The* pills?"

"Yes. *The* pills."

I could see the brown ring of rust where the Tylenol bottle used to sit, but the bottle itself was gone.

That was the only thing the burglar had taken, it seemed.

But how did this guy know about the pills? Why had he taken them *now*?

"You should go. I'll walk you to your car."

"And leave you wet, limping and burglarized? What kind of a friend would I be?"

She guided me to the houndstooth couch. We sat there listening to the rain *snick-snack* against the front windows. The El rumbled into its station, which sounded like thunder at first.

"I'm going to stay here tonight."

"There's no lock on the door. You can stay here. Anybody can stay here, help themselves to anything in the apartment. What does it matter?"

Her finger touched my chin, turned my face.

"Nobody else is welcome."

She kissed me.

We pushed the door shut to make sure it would at least stay closed, if not locked. We pulled out the houndstooth couch, made up the bed. We crawled in together and held each other, kissed each other, listened to the rain and the rumble of the El and kissed each other some more. We kissed until we faded into each other and it was hard to tell where I stopped and where she began and vice versa.

It was everything I'd wanted, but assumed I would never get.

At some point we fell asleep and then I woke up and gently touched the side of her face, just to feel her skin beneath my three good fingertips.

And then a harsh voice said:

"Hello, *Mickey*."

I COULD SEE NOTHING in the room. Just the streetlights, filtered through the front windows. Who was speaking?

Then, by my right ear: "Sorry I didn't come to the window. But I was sleeping. They make me sleep so much. But I woke up when I heard your voice. I've been waiting years to hear your voice."

I jolted and sat up in bed, looked around. And then I felt hands grab the sides of my head and pull me out of bed.

I'll admit it: I screamed.

Meghan woke up a nanosecond later, pushing herself up from the mattress. But something pushed her back down, violently. The springs of the couch strained beneath her.

"Stay out of this. This is family business, whore."

Then I saw him. He was a complete stranger, but I recognized the voice. It was older. It had deepened. But it was still the same voice.

Billy Allen Derace.

"Can you see me, Mickey?"

Yeah, I could see him.

But not quickly enough.

His fist smashed into my face quickly followed by his knee to my balls, which I swear came heaving out of nowhere. The lower half of my body exploded in white hot pain. My legs trembled for a second before giving out on me, and my knees slammed into the hardwood floor. Gravity wasn't working like it should. My internal compass was off—way, way off.

I crawled forward a few feet, the tips of my three good fingers clutching at the uneven spaces between the floorboards. My lip was throbbing and my balls felt like they were the size of cantaloupes. I crawled on a single elbow and both knees toward the bathroom. Anywhere.

Derace laughed at me. Walked toward me, ready to drag me back into the living room for more fun and games.

"Where you going, *Mickey*?"

Away from you.

"Would you rather me spend time with your girlfriend here? I like playing with the girls. Wig wam bam, gonna make you understand . . ."

Meghan screamed. I turned to see her lash out at the air. Her eyes popped open as something grabbed her throat. No.

"STAY AWAY FROM HER!"

I spun myself around and crawled back toward the couch.

"Wig wam bam, gonna getchoo if I can . . ."

Meghan cried out again but her voice was a weak rasp.

"But I think I'll save her for later. After I deal with you."

Something hard slammed into the side of my head. I think by chance I'd moved at the right moment, otherwise I would have been kicked in the face. I saw a white flash and collapsed to the ground, rolled over onto my back. I reached out with my three good fingers and tried to find the bathroom doorway so I could pull myself up.

Fingers tore at the back of my neck, then found the back of my head. There was a tug at the back of my waist . . . and then I was vertical again.

And then I was hurtling into the cherrywood desk. My face slammed against the back panel. My useless hand fumbled for the edge of the desk to anchor myself, but Derace was right behind me.

The next thing I knew the side of my face and my dead right shoulder slammed against the desk again, tilting onto two legs. Drawers opened, files gushed out.

Then he lifted me up and spun me around.

There was Billy Allen Derace. Nearly fifty years old. Wild red hair shaved down to nothing. Eyes sallow. Teary. Breath hot and stinking. I could feel him. I could smell him. He was standing behind me. This was no hallucination.

"Such a handsome face. That's not how I remember you. You had some scars. Nasty red-looking things. Maybe I'm supposed to give them to you."

"What do you want?"

"I was young when I killed your father. I was just starting out with the pills, figuring it all out. I thought the old man up here had some money I could steal, buy my own pills. But then I saw he had his own stash. And it was gooooooooood shit he had. Shit nobody else had. Shit that made me a superhero."

"You asshole—you killed my father."

"I was confused back then, you see. I thought he was you. I killed him because I thought he was you."

"What are you talking about?"

"Now I get what I want. Finally."

Then the hands released me.

"Hey. No. No no no no no no not yet . . ."

Billy was gone.

But I still heard his voice.

"DON'T YOU BASTARDS STICK THAT IN ME I'LL COME FOR ALL OF YOU IN YOUR SLEEP AND CUT YOU AND YOUR PRETTY LITTLE CHILDREN TO DEATH . . ."

My eyes may have been playing tricks. But for a flicker of a moment I saw the shape of Derace above me, and it was like he was wrestling with unseen forces, trying to lift his curled fists up, but he couldn't, because the man had invisible restraints around his wrists . . .

And then he vanished.

IN THE MID-1960S A professor at the University of Virginia ran a series of experiments on an advertising executive named Robert Monroe who claimed to have experienced numerous "out of body" (OBE) experiences. Monroe agreed to eight sessions in which he was placed in a locked room and asked to project himself. In two of those sessions Monroe was able to accurately describe the contents of another room in the facility in vivid detail.

In the late 1960s the Pentagon began a series of experiments aimed to control "remote viewing"—essentially, using psychics as spies to peer behind the Iron Curtain. Reportedly, the other side was engaged in similar experiments, resulting in a top secret, low-key "brain race" similar to the arms race and the moon race.

And in 1971, Dr. Mitchell DeMeo was given a government grant to find a way to induce an out-of-body experience using pharmaceuticals, which he'd developed over a period of twenty years.

DeMeo was affiliated with the prestigious Adams Institute. But he ran his experiments offsite; the board of directors at the Adams Institute thought it would be better that way. He used the address of the Papiro Center, at the time an empty building on the hospital's grounds that was sometimes used by the government, sometimes not. When it was not, unruly patients and "special cases" were housed in the center.

But DeMeo had actually set up shop in an abandoned apartment building on Frankford Avenue. They advertised in local papers for volunteers.

They accepted my father.

Dr. DeMeo hired a cleaning woman named Erna Derace to tidy up his office as well as the other apartments in the building. Payment was very modest, but in exchange, Erna was allowed to keep an apartment downstairs.

She had a boy named Billy. And he was instructed to be quiet at all times. In fact, their stay in the apartment was contingent on Billy "behaving."

NO ONE CARED ABOUT the experiments now, because the experiments were seen as a failure.

And the story had gone untold.

The story was all here in the papers, which had been buried in drawers of the cherrywood desk. Meghan had found the motherlode when she righted the desk after Billy Derace had tried to smash my head through it. Everything was in there. Grandpop Henry had clearly been through it all, and kept the relevant stuff neatly organized in the desk drawers. The boxes and crates were essentially leftovers. Trash he hadn't gotten around to bringing outside. We'd been looking in the wrong place this whole time.

Meghan flipped through DeMeo's experiment notes, all of which were neatly typewritten and separated into three categories: positive, negative and "questionable." The negative files were thick, and had taken up most of the drawer. The questionables were comparatively slim. And the positives were thinner still.

We more or less read in silence, as if we were both engrossed in the same 500,000-page novel that had gushed itself out of the desk. Only, we were on wildly different chapters, trying to piece together the story out of order. At one point Meghan looked up at me.

"Okay, so Dr. DeMeo was researching out-of-body experiences. As far as we know, Billy Derace is still locked up, under heavy sedation at the Adams Institute. So this means the Derace we saw last night was what . . . an astral projection?"

"Which will make it very interesting to explain to the police."

"True."

Then I thought this through a bit more.

"Wait wait wait—that doesn't make sense. Say he has the same pills I do. And let's say he can do the same things I can do. Does this mean he's come back from some future year just to mess with me now?"

"Maybe the whole going back in time thing is specific to you. According to these papers here, it was all about astral projection. Harnessing it. Making it predictable. Finding people who were predisposed to it. Maybe you, and maybe your father, could only project into the past."

"What makes you say that?"

Meghan held up the positive folder.

"Because in this folder is Dr. DeMeo's one proven success. And his name is Billy Allen Derace."

"You're kidding. He ran drug experiments on a twelve-year-old boy? The son of the woman he was banging?"

Meghan opened the folder, handed it to me.

"I don't think he was twelve. These notes are dated from early 1980. That would make Derace, what, eighteen years old then?"

I skimmed the notes. Meghan was right. Derace had been an

unqualified success. Able to walk around outside his body and identify objects in other rooms with ease. DeMeo was practically gushing. He also noted that his success was "no doubt linked to the extreme dosage administered to subject over a short period of time."

In short: Derace had been pumped full of these pills in order to make the out-of-body experience work.

But why do this to Billy? Had he volunteered? Had Erna coerced her son to do it to stay in the good graces of that fat pill-pusher?

Meghan found my father's page after a short while. He had been in the "questionable" folder, and it seemed that the pills had the same effect on the father as they did the son. He was hurled back in time, too, only to his birth year—1949. DeMeo's notes were snide, dismissive. My father insisted what he was seeing was real, and asked for more time to prove it. DeMeo let him have a few more sessions, then abruptly bounced him from the experiment. "Subject W. clearly wanted to milk the system for more money."

I shook my head.

"DeMeo didn't believe him. But my father was telling the truth."

Oh hell—my father.

Billy.

"What?"

The pallet full of cinder blocks that had been dangling over me finally broke free and smashed down on my head. I scrambled across the room, nearly tripping, and pulled out the death scrapbook Grandpop had made.

"Mickey, what is it?"

I flipped, found the *Bulletin* article. Billy Derace hadn't just disappeared from the scene of the crime. *He had never really been there.* It was his astral projection that had shown up, and it was strong enough and real enough to be seen and shown to a table and order a steak and a beer to bide his time. He'd ordered the steak because he wanted the knife. He couldn't bring one with him, because his physical body was locked up in the Adams Institute.

I don't know what I sounded like as I explained it to Meghan. It came out as a tumble of ideas and words. Somehow, though, it made sense to her. I think she was finally believing me—believing that those pills could do what I said they could.

"But what's the connection between Derace and your father? They were both experimented on, but eight years apart. What made Derace pick up a knife and stab him to death in a bar?"

"I don't know."

"I heard him talking to you last night. I heard him say, 'I killed him because I thought he was you.'"

"I have no idea."

AFTER A WHILE, MEGHAN hit my crappy laptop for some Google searches and we filled in some pieces that the notes from the desk couldn't. First, she found a death notice for DeMeo.

"Says here in the *Inquirer* that Dr. Mitchell DeMeo died in 2002. When did your grandpop move here?"

"A year later."

"Oh shit. He didn't just die. He was stabbed to death on Frankford Avenue at . . . Sellers Street? Is that nearby?"

"Just a few blocks away. Did you say stabbed?"

"He was walking to his car. Had the keys in his hand. Police say robbery wasn't a motive, as his car keys and his wallet were still on the body when he was found."

"Billy."

"Yeah, I'd say that was certainly a possibility."

Meghan kept typing; I kept digging. As a reporter I used to love printed sources. They were puzzle pieces. But now, there were too many pieces. Nothing seemed to match up or make sense.

"Um . . ."

"What?"

"I had somebody in my dad's office do a little checking for me—and he just e-mailed back. This building is still owned by the U.S. government. I think your grandpop was squatting. Which means that technically, *you're* squatting."

Somehow this news wasn't the crushing blow it should have been. I was already thinking that there was no way I'd be spending another night in this apartment. Not with Billy Derace knowing where to find me.

And Meghan.

A HALF HOUR LATER, dawn crept up over the Frankford skyline. We'd been digging and reading and throwing questions at each other all through the night. But now, with daylight here, I told Meghan she should probably go home.

"Are you kidding? Just when this is coming together?"

"It's not safe here."

"Don't tell me—Frankford's a bad neighborhood."

"You know that's not what I mean. I'm talking about Derace. Hell, I'm thinking about swallowing my pride, packing up my crap and asking my mom if I can crash in a spare bedroom for a few days. Just until I sort this stuff out."

"No way am I leaving you now."

"Seriously, Meghan, I'd feel a lot better if you kept your distance. I promise, I won't leave you out of this."

And I wouldn't. There was nothing I wanted more than Meghan to stay with me right now. To stay with me forever, actually. But I couldn't risk her life, not because of my selfishness. Billy Derace wouldn't know who she was, where she lived. To him, she was just another woman. The only connection he had to her was through me.

"I don't believe this. All of this time, and you push me away now? Seriously, Mickey—what the hell?"

She couldn't stay. She couldn't be anywhere near me. Not now.

"I'll call you."

When she left this time, she didn't kiss me. She made sure I saw her face for a moment, her angry eyes, and then she left.

The door snicked shut and I sat on the houndstooth couch, intending to close my eyes for just a minute. One minute I was staring at the cracks in the ceiling and the next utter exhaustion took over. I was out. Gone.

It was good to finally let go.

SOMETIME LATER—IT MUST have been early afternoon—my cell phone rang. Through a curtain of gray haze I saw the caller was Frankford Hospital. My mom was probably in my grandpop's room and wanted to bug me about visiting him. I let the call go to voice mail and rolled back over. Maybe the drool would run down the other cheek, even things out. A while later the phone rang again. Please stop, Mom. Let me enjoy my coma here in peace. Then again. And a fourth time. So I finally picked up the phone and called into voice mail to see what the big panic was about . . .

But it wasn't my mother. It was Grandpop Henry, calling from the hospital. I redialed the number. He answered.

"Mickey?"

"Grandpop? You're awake?"

"Yeah, I'm awake. Been awake for a while. I need you to come here right away."

XI

THE NIGHT WATCHMAN

GRANDPOP HENRY WAS COVERED in blankets. A catheter tube ran down the side of the bed to a plastic container, but it was only partially obscured by a thin piece of blue linen. His piss was on display for the world to see.

He looked at me and I swear he had tears in his eyes.

"Your arm."

His voice was croaky and weak. I looked down at my right arm in its sling.

"I'm fine. It's nothing. And hey, you're the one in the hospital, remember?"

"You got that going back, didn't you?"

"That happened to you, too, huh?"

"I haven't been able to move my left arm for two years. But never mind that. Tell me everything you did. There isn't much time."

"What I did?"

"Yeah, I could hear you just fine last time you were here. You found the pills."

"How about you start telling me everything *you* did, Grandpop? Because I've spent the past week trying to figure it all out."

"There's no time for that. I need to make sure you didn't screw anything up."

Oh, that was rich. *Me* screwing things up? I didn't

want to stand here and be lectured. I wanted to know what this was all about. All of my life, my family had been talking around me instead of to me. I was sick of it.

"No."

"What do you mean, no?"

I looked him in the eyes.

"I'm not telling you a thing until you explain everything to me."

"Feh."

"I want you to say the words. You were trying to go back in time to kill Billy Derace, the man who killed your son. My father."

"Don't be ridiculous."

"You're denying it?"

"Yes, I'm denying it. Actually, I was going back in time to kill Billy Derace's father."

"AFTER YOUR FATHER WAS killed there was no trial. Nobody could place Derace at the bar, so he stayed where he was—that loony bin up the road. Well, that wasn't good enough for me. I wanted to look into his eyes, to know if he'd done it or not. Then I'd do what I had to. But I knew I'd never be able to set foot within a mile of that place if I told them who I really was."

"So you got a job there."

"Hey. Who's telling this, you or me? So yeah, I got a job there. This was years later—1989. But before that I waited. Paid attention to the newspapers, just in case they were to spring him early. I read all the local papers cover to cover looking for any mention of him. I saw all the pieces about those tramps he murdered—but I had no idea it was him. Nobody did. Nobody *does*. You wrote that story a few years ago—"

"You read that?"

"Yeah, I read it, I read everything you wrote in that paper, even the things you got wrong, and you got plenty wrong. Now will you stop interrupting me? I don't have that much time. Anyway, you wrote that story a few years ago and by then I knew, I knew what he'd been up to because I was living there and I found DeMeo's notes and then I knew what he could do."

"DeMeo was killed in 2002."

"Yeah, by that shadowy son of a bitch. I'm not crying for him, though. DeMeo deserved what he got. He knew about the hooker murders, but didn't say anything because he thought Billy was his big breakthrough. After all those years of pumping people with that poison, he finally finds somebody who can do this cockamamie walking out of your body stunt. Only problem is, it's this nut-job kid who raided his drug stash when his whore mother wasn't looking."

"Erna Derace."

"Erna Derace, yeah. DeMeo's journal said—"

"Wait. We didn't find any journal. We looked all through the desk and didn't find any journal."

"I know. 'Cause I burned it. Once I figured it out, I didn't want nobody seeing this stuff. Nobody's business but mine. Now. You're my grandson, you're the only flesh and blood thing on this earth that I care about, but if you don't shut up and let me tell this story I swear to God I'm going to pop you in the kisser."

"Sorry."

"Sorry, sorry, yeah, we're all sorry. Anyway, it was around 1980 and this kid, Billy, had grown up to be a real piece of trash. He's drinking at thirteen, doing the dope when he's fourteen, stealing shit and mugging people when he's seventeen. By that time, he also starts breaking into DeMeo's office, hoping to score pills. He scored pills all right."

"Wait—he started back then?"

"He started back then. He realized what he could do. I went back to those papers and read about all of these little break-ins up and down Frankford Avenue back in 1979. A real one-man crime wave. Nobody could figure it out. But I did. Only, it was too late to do anything about it."

I thought about my first experiences with the pill, and yeah, even my mind went to larceny. I was a thirty-seven-year-old guy with a fairly decent moral compass. Billy Derace, though, was an abused kid with a mother who drank and whored herself out to the fat doctor upstairs and pretty much felt the deck stacked against him. Of course he would goof around on those pills. He must have felt like a superhero with new powers. Only he didn't go back in time. He was able to astrally project into the present. He could do whatever he wanted.

One thing didn't make sense though.

"So why did he kill Dad?"

Grandpop looked at me, annoyed.

"Because he was a nut, why else? Like I was saying, I started working at the hospital in 1993. They did a background check, but it wasn't a very good one, because they didn't know I had a son. I'd been divorced since 1959, so I guess they didn't dig back too far. And your dad was using that stupid name, so no one put it together. Anyway, by that time DeMeo already had Derace over in this maximum security wing—"

"How did Derace end up there in the first place?"

"He overdosed in the summer of 1979. And surprise, surprise, the crime wave ended. His mom begged DeMeo to put him somewhere safe, not turn him over to a state-run hospital. I guessed it worked, because he had his own bed over at the loony bin."

"So he *was* at the Adams Institute when my dad was killed."

"Yeah. Only he wasn't. I think he started going for walks outside his body full-time, since his own body was more or less out of the picture. Like me."

I looked at my grandpop.

"Like you?"

"I haven't been sleeping this whole time. I've been walking."

"Walking where?"

"Just walking. Never mind that. You wanted to hear this whole thing, fine. I understand. And you know, it's probably a good thing someone else knows, in case I'm not able to fix things. But for now, really, Mickey, I want you to shut up and let me tell this the way I want to tell it before I strangle you with my pee tube.

"Okay, Grandpop."

"SO I STARTED WORKING there and learned that this little bastard's kept at the Papiro Center. Nobody was allowed in except DeMeo and his own cleaning staff, twenty-four/seven lockdown. The cleaning staff was allowed on the grounds, you know, to cut the grass and sweep up, but we were never allowed in the building. I spent years trying to get into that building. They had their own cleaning people. Bused in from somewhere else, I don't know where. So it became a matter of stealing some keys. I figured I'd hang on to the job long enough to steal some keys and get myself into that building and grab a pillow and push it down over his face until he stopped breathing. Or maybe I'd bring a steak knife with me. Stab the bastard, just like he stabbed your father. Watch the hot blood splatter against his face as he looked into mine. Then I wouldn't care what the cops did to me. They could throw me in a cell, do whatever the hell they wanted. But I never got in. Instead, I was reading the paper one day when I saw that DeMeo had been found, knifed in the back and in the head. I thought maybe that creepy little bastard had gotten loose, killed his own doctor, was ready to go on a rampage. But no. According to the patient logs, Billy was still in lockdown. He hadn't moved. He'd been strapped to his bed. I couldn't figure it out. It made no sense. When DeMeo bought it, I dug up his personnel file and found another address— the place on Frankford Avenue. I didn't think I had much time, so I broke in, figuring I'd get a few hours, maybe a day before they clear out all of this stuff. I start looking through his papers, none of it makes a damn bit of sense. I stay there that one night, just to give me a little time to look around, and then I end up staying the next night. Nobody ever shows. So I end up staying there for good. The *mushin* running the store downstairs was paying his rent to De-Meo in cash, sticking it in his mailbox, so I took the money and paid the bills with it. I spent my time looking through his papers. And then I started reading about his pills. Crazy horseshit, I know, but there was a ton about them. How he thought they could give people out-of-body experiences. He never had much luck. They didn't work on very many people. And half of those people didn't even have real out-of-body experiences. They said they were back in some other time only they were invisible. So I found his stash of pills in the medicine cabinet and took one, just to see what the fuss was about. Only later did I put it all together. Of course DeMeo had no idea. His patients there started describing stuff from twenty, thirty, forty years in the past, and he thought they were making it all up. But I knew. I knew the very first time I took those things. Because I took one and I went into the past. I saw things I never thought I'd see again. The Starr Café, right there on the corner of Margaret and Frankford. It closed when I was a kid, but suddenly there I was looking in the front window. I couldn't be-lieve it. So I took more pills and started walking around more. I learned quick that I could only walk at night. You discovered the same thing yourself, I see. But the nights were long, and there was so much I wanted to see. I walked down to the river and saw the Delaware River Bridge, almost finished. They opened it the year I was born—1926. They call it the Ben Franklin Bridge now, but it was the Delaware River Bridge then, and it was the most beautiful thing you'd ever seen. I saw my father and my mother down on Second Street. You never met my father, because he died when I was just a kid. I hadn't laid eyes on him for seventy some years. I was a ghost but I didn't care. I was seeing everything I'd missed."

"I know what you mean."

"You went back to your birth year, too, didn't you? I don't know why that is. The pills only do that to very, very few people—I read DeMeo's reports. But I guess that's how our brains were built. We take these pills, we go back. And when I saw my father, and myself as a baby, I started thinking of your father. Thinking maybe it wasn't too late. Thinking maybe I could do something to fix things. I couldn't do a thing about Billy Derace. He wouldn't be born for another twenty-four years. But I could find his father. I could find his father and do something about him."

"You never found him, though."

"Victor Derace didn't exist back then. It's like he was a ghost."

"Billy's mom told me he changed his name a lot. But he was born Victor D'Arrazzio."

My grandpop stopped and looked at me. Really looked at me. His jaw opened a little, and then he moistened his lips and looked over at his right hand, which was clutching the blanket.

"D'Arrazzio."

"Yeah."

"Spell it."

I did the best I could, but Erna hadn't spelled it for me either.

Grandpop didn't say anything for a while, and when he spoke, he was mostly muttering to himself.

"So it's not too late."

THE WHOLE TIME GRANDPOP was speaking—and it was just like the old family holidays, Mickey sit down and shut up, Mickey go get your grandfather another warm beer—I took everything in. But with each new piece, I thought of my father. He'd taken the pills, too.

And the more I stared at Grandpop, and at his thin, mangled fingers from years of manual labor, taped up with IV tubes, I started to realize what else had happened.

The story didn't begin with Billy Allan Derace attacking my father at random in December 1980. The story also began with my father taking those pills in 1972 and being thrown back into his own past. I remembered what my mom had told me, about what my dad had said not long after I was born.

Why he wouldn't speak to my grandfather.

Why he hated him.

And quite possibly why he'd been so distant with me.

He didn't know how to be with me.

All he knew was what his father had taught him.

I TOUCHED GRANDPOP'S HAND. It was cold and dry. He snapped out of his reverie and looked up at me.

"What?"

"Did my dad ever talk to you about those experiments when he was alive?"

"No. We didn't talk much then. I didn't know how to talk to him. He didn't seem to want to talk to me either."

"Did you ever wonder why?"

"What are you talking about?"

"You went back to 1926—the year you were born. I went back to 1972—the year I was born. So when my dad went back to 1949, what did he see?"

"How the hell would I know?"

"You would know because *you were there*. You were there in 1949, not long after my dad was born, and you were smacking Grandmom around with a belt."

His eyes bulged—I caught him by surprise. Then they narrowed into hot angry slits.

"You don't know what you're talking about."

"No, I do, and you're going to listen to me now. Don't you realize that dad took those pills, too? He probably went back and did the same things you and I did. He went home. But what did he see? Well, I guess he saw how you really were. Smacking Grandmom around."

"You don't understand a goddammed thing. You don't have any kids."

"Yeah, and with shining examples like you and my dad, why the hell would I? Raise them, hold them, cuddle them, just so I can turn around and start beating them on the ass with a leather belt? Beat them until the backs of their legs are black and blue, and thank God it's still long pants weather so no one at school will see?"

My grandpop said nothing for a while, staring up at the ceiling. Finally, after a while, he spoke again.

"Well, you won't have to worry about it anymore."

"What do you mean?"

"I mean, I'm going to go back and fix things."

"Right. With those magic pills. But I don't think you're going to be able to fix things, because no matter how hard you push, life has a way of pushing back even harder."

"I can fix things."

"No, you actually can't. The pills are gone. Someone stole them."

"Yeah, I know. *I* stole them."

"What? That was you? How?"

"I hired some kid I know to break into the place, which technically isn't breaking in, since it's my place."

"No it's not. It belongs to the government."

"Yeah and the government owes me for what it did to my family. They couldn't kill my boy in Vietnam, so they had to get him with a bunch of loony pills. Well, I'm going to use those pills against the sons of bitches. I'm going to set things right."

My grandpop had them in his hand. He forced the pills into his mouth and chewed on them like hard candy.

I LUNGED FOR HIM, forgetting that I was down to three good fingers, and they weren't enough. He was eighty-four yet still strong as an ox. A lifetime of manual labor will do that for you.

He smiled at me as he chewed, pale eyes boring into mine.

"Don't worry. You're not going to remember any of this."

Even now, he couldn't bear to call me by my name. Mickey. He'd never liked it. Never liked that my dad had named me after a faggy fat-lipped singer in a rock and roll band.

"It doesn't work that way! You can't change the past. I've tried. It doesn't work!"

"You just didn't try hard enough."

"What do you mean, I didn't try hard enough? What did you

want me to do, go back in time and kill a twelve-year-old kid? Is that what I should have done? Is that what you're trying to do? Grandpop, you can't just do that! You can't!"

But I was talking to his unconscious body. His eyes were already closed; his other self had already left his body behind.

XII

HOW IT ENDS

THE SUMMER SUN BURNED at the back of my neck and the top of my head as I walked home from the hospital. Where was my fedora now? At home, in the apartment.

I wanted to blow the last of my money drowning myself in beer, but I wanted it to be good beer. After all, it was time to celebrate, right? My grandpop just O.D.-ed on a bottle of time-traveling pills and was going to fix everything. So I stepped into the bodega and went straight to the counter.

"Do you sell Sierra Nevada?"

The guy behind the counter looked at me.

"Eh, no. Bud, Coors Light, Yuengling, Old English."

"No microbrews? Really?"

"Hey, I like the stuff, too. But it'd never sell in this neighborhood. Aren't you the guy who's been buying up all of the Golden Anniversary?"

"Yeah."

"And you live upstairs, don't you."

"Yeah."

He held out his hand.

"Willie Shahid."

"Mickey Wade."

"Not that it's any of my business, but where's the cranky guy who used to live upstairs?"

"That would be my grandpop. You two didn't get along?"

"Well, being called a *mushin* kind of puts a strain on the relationship. And I don't even know what a *mushin* is."

"It's probably what you think it is."

"Yeah, I figured. Look, this is also none of my business, but do you have any friends staying over? I thought I heard some noises upstairs earlier."

"I don't think so. Could be my friend Meghan—the attractive young lady you may have seen me here with a while back. Or it could be one of the other residents."

"Other residents? You're the only one who lives upstairs."

"I'm what?"

"Yeah. Didn't your grandfather tell you?"

"The rest of the apartments are vacant?"

"Have been ever since I opened this place five years ago."

I KEYED MY WAY into the front door and was preparing to bound up the stairs when I heard a moaning noise. A woman's voice. At first I thought it was Erna. Then I remembered no, it couldn't be. This was 2009, not 1972.

Then it hits me, who else it could be.

No no no . . .

I don't remember climbing the two flights. I just remember fumbling with my keys before remembering the lock was broken. I kicked open the door to the apartment. It was empty. No one on the couch, or in the bathroom, or under the desk or in the closet. I ran back out into the hallway. Hearing another moan.

I tried 3-B, which was locked. Now I did kick in the door, which opened a lot easier than I would have thought. Maybe it was the adrenaline, but more likely this building was outfitted with shitty doors back when Dr. DeMeo turned it into his little science lab.

Inside, 3-B was a frozen apartment setting, like a page out of a 1970s Sears catalog. Spare. Table, chairs, cheesy tablecloth with an awful paisley pattern. Three candlesticks. A plastic apple, a plastic set of grapes, and two plastic pears, arranged not in a bowl but at random on the table. The dust in here was unreal. I think I was the first person to set foot in this room in about thirty years.

At least, a physical foot.

By the time I kicked open 3-C and yelled for Meghan, pleaded with her to keep moaning, I could hear her, I realized what this was. His test control rooms. That's why he needed an empty apartment building. His OBE subjects would lie on that psychiatrist's couch of his and try to astrally project themselves into other rooms. If they made it, he or she would be asked to describe the contents of the room. One apple, doctor. Two pears. And the ugliest tablecloth I've ever seen.

"MEGHAN!"

Another moan—down on the second floor.

But now I knew where she'd be. She'd be in Erna and Billy's old apartment—2-C.

Because Billy would have dragged her there.

SHE WAS ON THE floor of the empty apartment, trembling. She was covered in too much blood for me to see her wounds. Some of the blood had dried on the floor. She'd been here for a long time.

"Meghan stay with me, it's going to be okay, the hospital's just a few blocks away, I'm calling now, Meghan come on, look at me, I'm here, it'll be okay."

She mumbled.

I could barely make out the words.

Waiting for me.

Hallway.

He'd been waiting for her in the hallway, just before sunrise.

I fumbled with the phone. I don't remember what I said to the 911 dispatcher, other than a woman's been stabbed, please hurry, get here right now, please, God, PLEASE, followed by the address and the apartment number. I gave them Willie Shahid's name downstairs.

I didn't know first aid, other than to try to apply direct pressure and try to stop the flow of blood. But where was I supposed to start? Horrible gashes and scars covered Meghan's face and arms, her pretty, elegant hands. The knife had slashed through her blouse, too, a number of times.

All I could do was watch her neck as it still trembled slightly—faint proof of life. All I could do was lie to her.

"Meghan you're going to be okay," I said. "The ambulance is on its way. The hospital is only a few blocks away. You're going to be fine. Just a few scratches."

It was all I could do.

NO.

That *wasn't* all I could do.

I reached into my pocket. I still had one half of a pill from last night—when I was parked outside the Adams Institute and tried to wake up Billy Derace.

I swallowed it, closed my eyes, feeling the burn in my blood.

BILLY WAS PLAYING WITH a G.I. Joe doll when I kicked in his front door. I held a steak knife with the three fingers of my good hand.

All I had to do was stick it in his chest to the hilt and hold it there with my left hand until he stopped moving. Then I would leave. I wouldn't have to worry about wiping the blade clean, or removing fingerprints from the handle. No forensics team was going to track me down. I wouldn't have to burn my clothes.

I would just have to kill Billy.

Kill little Billy Derace, and life resets itself.

Meghan lives.

It was daylight, but I was being smart about it—wearing Grandpop's overcoat, shoes and gloves. I also pulled a wool ski cap over my face. It was hard to breathe, and it partially blinded me, but I could still see through the loose gaps in the weave. I put the fedora on my head for extra protection. I didn't care if the sun found me and nuked me to pieces. I just needed to kill Billy first.

Billy knew it, too.

"Mom!"

He screamed, and I couldn't blame him. I would be terrified out of my mind, too, if a ghost wearing a face mask and a fedora kicked in my front door. But I didn't give a shit. I whipped my three-fingered fist across his face. His little head snapped back, banging against the doors of a small hutch. Is this what it felt like to hit a kid, Erna? Was it a thrill to know that you were older, stronger and more vicious, and no matter what, this little boy had to take it?

The hutch doors popped loose from their magnetic locks and swung open slightly. Billy recovered quickly, though—kids often do—and scrambled across the dirty carpet, heading for the apartment door.

But I was older. Smarter. And I had the advantage of not being terrified. I made three quick leaps across the room and beat him there, kicking the door shut with my knee. The slam was like a rifle shot echoing throughout the stairwell.

"Mom!" he screamed again.

I placed my foot against his small chest and pushed hard. Not hard enough to break ribs, but enough to knock the air out of him. It's funny, you calling for your mother now, little Billy. Think she's going to come and save you, or join in? Maybe I'm doing her a favor. Maybe you did ruin her life.

You've ruined mine.

Now I had him where I wanted him. All I had to do was stick the knife in his chest to the hilt and hold it there until he stopped moving.

I had the knife out now, my three good fingers grasping the black plastic handle. Then I straddled Billy, my legs on either side of his chest. He was crying and screaming, hot fat tears running down the sides of his face. His skin was bright red.

"You didn't give me a choice," I said.

But he wasn't listening. He was too insane with fear, not knowing where to turn or how to protect himself or call for help. Because now he'd realized that help was *not* coming. He shook his head back and forth as if he could shake himself out of this nightmare.

The knifepoint was just a few inches above his heaving chest.

All I had to do was stick in the knife and hold it there until he stopped moving.

Think about it as a dream, I told myself.

A nightmare.

A nightmare you *can* wake from.

It was as if Billy could read my mind; he knew what I was planning. This was not a normal beating. There would be no wiping the blood away, putting a Band-Aid over the wound. There would be no bruises that slowly fade until you're no longer embarrassed to wear shorts outside. This would be the ultimate hurt, the final punishment for being a bad boy.

So he started slamming me with his small fists, desperately pounding at my chest and stomach. His body squirmed beneath my legs. I was focused on the knife in my hand and tried to will myself to plunge it down. Billy got lucky. He reached up and grabbed a fistful of my ski mask and yanked down, exposing my face.

"YOU!"

He saw me. He recognized me.

"I KNEW IT WAS YOU! WHY ARE YOU DOING THIS TO ME?"

Why *was* I doing this to him?

And then I finally put the last piece together.

Billy Derace didn't have a grudge against my father. They hadn't met one day in 1972. Billy Derace grew up wanting to kill my father because of what I was doing right now, right this very instant. He'd been scared to death as a twelve-year-old by a man wearing a mask and he'd ripped away the mask and grew up terrified of that face and then later, after years of abuse and drugs and time-traveling pills, he'd gone looking for the face that terrified him.

My face.

But in 1980, the closest thing he could find was my father.

I WAS MY FATHER'S killer.

I LET BILLY GO. I dropped the knife. I climbed to my feet. I left through the front door. I climbed the stairs. I heard a door slam down on the ground floor. Billy cried out for his mother. His mother cried back, an awful shriek that echoed through the stairwell. There was the urgent clacking of high heels up the stairs but I didn't care. I just wanted to go back into the office and collapse and close my eyes.

THE DAYLIGHT IN THE hallway scorched the skin on my face. It felt like the worst sunburn I've ever had.

I kicked in the door, just like I'd kicked in all the others in this building. There was a complete set now.

I collapsed to the ground, then got up on all fours. The half pill I'd swallowed was already wearing off. I felt dizzy.

Then Erna stepped through the open doorway, holding the gun.

"You hateful son of a bitch," she said, then squeezed the trigger.

The slug sliced through my astral body and buried itself in the floor beneath me. I felt a searing pain in my abdomen, even though there was no entry wound, no blood.

I didn't say anything.

She fired again, twice, and both shots were like hot needles in my chest, each stabbing me through my pectoral muscles. The pain made my eyes water. I dropped to my knees and lifted my left hand—the one with only three fingers.

"I'm going to kill you."

I shook my head.

"It's no use. You can't, because I'm not actually here."

"You're not making any sense."

Erna squatted next to me and lifted me up by the lapels of my borrowed overcoat. Her knuckles were raw, fingers bony. I'd never noticed how thin her hands were. It must hurt to be slapped by those hands.

I looked up at her.

"You think I'm dead but I'm not. I'm alive in the future. I just visit the past. So believe me when I tell you that unless you help your son, he's going to grow up to hurt a lot of people. A lot of innocent people. He's going to be a killer, Erna, unless you pull your head out of your ass and be a mother to him."

"You're from the devil! You're here to torment me and my boy!"

"Today is June 18, 2009. My real body is laying in this apartment in the future. Billy's in a mental hospital. You're living on the streets, and you're a goddamned mess."

She repeated the date to herself.

"June 18, 2009."

It couldn't make sense to her. It must sound like the title of a science fiction movie.

I tried to make her understand.

"So you can't kill me. It's not even worth trying. But you can try to save your son."

She dropped me. My head hit the floor with a thump. She didn't quite react at first. My words had to be picked apart, analyzed.

Then she looked down at me, deranged smile on her face, and said: "No . . . I know how to kill you."

And then she began to rip the brown paper from the office windows.

SUNSHINE SMASHED THROUGH THE windows, washing over my entire body. My overcoat began to sizzle and then fade away. My eyes burned as if I'd looked directly into the sun through a twin pair of high-powered telescopes. The skin of my face was beyond fevered; it was ablaze.

My ears functioned long enough to hear Erna ripping the rest of the brown paper from the windows. The nerves under my skin sensed the additional heat and light, and they curled up and withered inside my body.

And then I was gone.

I WOKE UP IN the same position on the floor. Belly down. Head turned to one side. Drool coming out of my mouth.

I don't know how long I'd been there, or how long I would be there, because I was completely paralyzed, top of my head to my feet. Just like my fingers, just like my right arm, I knew my body was still there, every piece of it. But I had zero control over any of it.

I could die here.

I could die here and no one would know.

MANY HOURS, I THINK, passed before the door creaked open behind me. I heard heavy footsteps.

"Hello, you bastard. It's June 18, 2009."

Oh God. No.

She showed herself to me first. She wanted to make sure I knew it was her, so I knew who'd be doing this to me. It was Erna, the bag lady from Frankford Avenue. Which was where she'd ended up after watching her son institutionalized, and her lover knifed to death under the El. She'd been crazy back in 1972, and the intervening years hadn't done much to improve the situation.

But what made her real crazy, I realized now, were all the dead people she saw walking through her apartment and the empty apartments she cleaned. They'd make faces at her, because they were just goofing around, having fun. Dr. DeMeo's patients, in their past and some even propelled forward into the future a few years. And she thought she was losing her mind, but was afraid to tell the doctor, because then she'd lose her place and her job and then what would they do? So she said nothing and she drank wine and tried to forget about all the dead people.

Except the one dead person who'd told her the truth. That he was actually alive, in another year altogether. He'd even helpfully supplied the date.

So Erna Derace had waited.

And on June 18, 2009, she went back to that apartment building.

And she used the last three bullet in the gun she'd been saving for thirty-seven years.

"Do you understand now?"

She shot me in the back three times, right between the shoulder blades.

WILLIE SHAHID, OWNER OF the bodega downstairs, heard sharp cracks, three in a row, then heard someone rumbling down the steps and out the front door. He made it out in time to see an old woman go shuffling down Frankford Avenue. What was that about, he must have wondered. Then he locked the front doors of his shop and walked upstairs to check it out, cell phone in hand.

Willie stood outside my apartment door—3-A. He knocked and waited. Something wasn't right. He sniffed the air; the acrid scent of chalk and burnt paper filled his nostrils. *Gunpowder.* It wasn't an unfamiliar scent to Willie Shahid. Not in this neighborhood.

So Willie flipped open his cell and dialed 911, giving the address and even the floor.

A short while later the EMTs arrived, and then three squad cars from the Philly PD, 15th District.

The EMTs moved me to a stretcher and carried me out the front door of the building, under the rumbling El train.

But by that time, I was already dead.

(XIII)

MY OTHER LIFE

SEE THAT BODY ON the mortician's slab, waiting to be pumped with formaldehyde and other assorted preserving chemicals?

That's me.

I don't know how long I've been dead, but I have to presume it's been a day or so. As I said at the beginning, when you're dead everything seems to happen all at once. Time's arrow only appears to fly straight when you're alive. Dead is something else. Once you cross that invisible line, you see things how they really are.

I am discorporated from my body. I am able to see everything I've done since birth, throughout my childhood, up through my adolescence and into adulthood.

But the strange thing is I don't quite remember any of it.

THERE'S ME, BALANCING ON the edge of the couch, arms and legs extended like I'm a superhero with the ability to fly. There's me, fighting with my brother, wrestling around on the floor like I'm Spider-Man and he's the Hulk and . . .

See that? My *brother*.

I don't remember having a brother.

But somehow, I do.

In this life I also seem to have two sisters—one ten years younger, and another twelve years younger. Their names are on the tip of my tongue, but I can't bring myself to speak them out loud. They're familiar and unfamiliar at the same time. I know them, I don't know them.

I STILL HAVE A father.

There he is, trying to teach me how to play guitar. Three small fingers on the fret board, struggling to form a C chord, the home base of all rock guitar chords, the first thing you learn.

Then there he is, teaching me what little he knows about the piano, because he decided he could use a keyboard player in the band rather than a second guitarist.

There's me, playing along on my first "gig" with my father when I'm nine years old.

There's me, playing a wedding with my father's band. I am fifteen, and my father is still alive. We're wearing tuxedo shirts and cummerbunds.

He's alive! How is this possible?

But sure enough, there's my father, in a suit, at my high school graduation. I want to be a writer, but music's a way to make money for now. I write my stories on my own time. I spent my weekends practicing and playing gigs. Eventually I quit the band and go off into journalism. I only play the piano once in a great while, but I listen to music all the time.

I pluck a thousand memories at random from a life I don't fully remember having lived.

I remember it all and I don't remember it at the same time.

· · ·

I AM STILL DEAD, but I am also alive. There's another me out there, living a life where my father never died.

The other me is married.

He's married to a young teacher named Meghan. Her father's a powerful Center City attorney. She's cut her beautiful long blond hair short.

We have two children.

I KEEP THINKING I'M going to wake up any minute now. But will I still be dead when I wake up?

AFTER A WHILE IT occurs to me that the way this unremembered life makes any sense is that Grandpop Henry succeeded in going back and changing something.

Something huge. Something reality-warping. Something that's rewoven the fabric of many lives. My life. My father's. Meghan's. The siblings I didn't know existed. Everyone's life has changed now. Everyone's taken two steps to the right and carried on as if their other lives never happened.

I even wonder, briefly, where Whiplash Walt is right now. Married to another client? Because Anne, my mother, is still married to my father. She quit smoking a few years ago because of our children. Children I didn't know we had. I grew up in a house full of cigarette smoke, but in the years since she's read a few things. She knows how deadly it is. So she quit.

I PLUCK OUT OTHER memories. I'm dead. I'm allowed to do this.

In this other life Erna Derace is childless. She never met Victor, she never had to experience the hell of burying her own child, never had to inflict living hell upon her other child. She leads a quiet lonely life. She never moves away from Frankford. Maybe she was never meant to have kids. Or maybe she was meant to have kids but screwed it up and is being punished in this alternate life. I catch glimpses of her, now and again, shopping on Frankford Avenue but I don't know who she is and she ignores me, too.

I SCAN THIS OTHER, alien life, looking for Grandpop Henry.

And all at once, of course—because everything happens all at once when you're dead—I pluck out the details of his altered life story.

Seems I've never met Grandpop Henry, in this version.

I'm able to go back and watch him beat my grandmother. They both drink too much. They argue a lot. They both married young, Grandpop just a year out of the service, and they're still figuring each other out. Then she gets pregnant with my father. Now he's married young and saddled with a kid he didn't particularly ask for and it makes him angry and it's stupid but he takes it out on her. He works a lot. He says it's to make them money, but it's more to avoid her.

In the late 1950s, when my father is only ten years old, Grandpop Henry gets into a bar fight at a joint under the Frankford El. The guy comes out of nowhere, starts hacking away at Grandpop. The assailant's name was Victor D'Arrazzio. Later, he would change it to "Vic Derace." According to his FBI rap sheet, D'Arrazzio liked cheap sweet wine, BBQ ribs and prostitutes.

Grandpop Henry was stabbed seventeen times, in the chest and throat. He died at the scene. It was declared a senseless killing.

My grandmom doesn't remember the beatings. She misses her husband. She mourns the life they could have had together.

D'Arrazzio kills himself a few years later, in state prison.

I grow up never having met Grandpop Henry.

IN THIS OTHER LIFE, the Frankford Slasher still killed women under the El during the late 1980s.

Only, it was somebody else doing the slashing.

BY THE TIME I was born, Grandpop Henry was long gone. Right now I remember him, and I don't remember him. I'm named for him. My father was thinking about musicians, but my mother suggested Henry. After his own father. The father he barely knew.

My name is Henry Wadcheck.

I remember him, and I don't remember him.

I want to remember him.

I need to remember him.

But I don't think I'll be allowed to remember him for very long.

And this is because my death is almost over, and in my original life, my grandpop's eighty-four-year-old body is about to give up and take its last breath. Everything's exploding out of that moment. My vision is blurring. I know what happens next, because when you're dead everything happens at once. That doesn't mean I experience life in one quick burst—like the old cliché about it flashing before your eyes. No, I relive every second. I retake every breath. I feel every cut, I savor every kiss. But I still know everything that is happening, did happen and will happen.

I knew everything the moment I started telling you this story.

I saw it all because I was dead.

But now I'm alive.

SO I'M ABOUT TO forget everything.

I told you this story because I so badly want to remember, even though I know it's impossible. You tell stories because you want some part of you to live on. And I know that's impossible.

I know that because right now I'm going to wake up.

WHEN I WAKE UP Meghan is already propped up on one elbow, beautiful eyes wide open, staring at me. I reach out and touch her face—her perfect, beautiful face. Even after two kids, even after twelve years of marriage, she's as gorgeous as ever. I love the feeling of her soft skin beneath my fingertips.

I'm pretty hungover.

Hot waves of sunshine burst through our windows. It's a humid Sunday morning—the first day of summer. I rub the sleep out of my eyes and tell her I dreamed about something, and it was one of those annoying, busy dreams where you're working so hard at something . . . but I can't remember a thing about it. So frustrating.

Then the kids come screaming into the room and jump on our bed and my daughter pushes a stuffed animal in my face and says *kissy! kissy!* So I kiss the stuffed animal—a bunny. They're loud. They're not going to let us sleep. They're also not going to allow us to fool around. They want one thing: us up.

They also have drawings in their hands, which puzzles me until I remember: it's Father's Day.

My dad's coming over later. Meghan's, too. I'm going to be on grill duty. I really should have more sleep if I'm going to be putting up with both sets of parents today . . .

But you know, whatever. I smile at my kids. They're beautiful, just like their mother.

I GO INTO THE bathroom to wash my face. My head's throbbing like crazy—Meghan and I had more than a few glasses of wine last night, and then we got friendly on the living room floor. I'm paying for it this morning, though. I open the medicine cabinet door.

There's a bottle of Tylenol inside. I don't recognize it. Bottle looks old, but I'm sure the pills inside are fine. Meghan wouldn't buy out-of-date medicine. Probably just an old container.

I tap two into my palm.

NOTES AND THANKS

THIS BOOK WOULDN'T EXIST if it weren't for Laura Lippman and Ilena Silverman. For the past few years the *New York Times Magazine* has been running a "Sunday Serial," featuring short novels from writers such as Elmore Leonard (who wrote the first, *Comfort to the Enemy*), Ian Rankin, Michael Connelly, and Laura Lippman.

Not long into her own serial, *The Girl in the Green Raincoat*, Laura recommended me to her editor, Ilena, for a possible future serial.

So one hot afternoon in September 2008 I received a call on my cell phone from the *New York Times*.

I thought it was about my subscription, so I almost didn't answer. But if there was a problem with my credit card, I'd rather know about it now.

Ilena introduced herself, and explained the concept of the Sunday serial—though she didn't have to. I've been a huge fan since that first Elmore Leonard installment. And I began my *Times* subscription when Connelly's serial (*The Overlook*) began, because I wanted to save the entire run. Yes, I'm a mystery nerd that way.

Then she asked me if I'd consider pitching something. I tried to play it cool, but I think I yelped the word *yes* before she even finished the question.

Everything about this excited me, but especially the form:

40,000 words, told in 15 installments, about 2,600 words each. True serial, with cliffhangers and everything, running in one of the best magazines in the world.

Did I pitch her? I pitched like you wouldn't believe.

I submitted four ideas to Ilena, but I knew the one I had my heart set on. It was a strange one, closer in spirit to my first novel, *Secret Dead Men*, than anything I'd written lately. In fact, at one point I'd planned *Expiration Date* as the follow up to *Secret Dead Men*. (Back then, though, I was calling it *The Dark Office*. Which is a title I didn't like much even back then.)

Ilena could tell I was excited about the first idea—the one I had my heart set on. So she invited me to write a short synopsis. So I wrote a synopsis. Then a long treatment/outline. Then, finally, a full three-thousand-word installment, just to show Ilena and Gerry Marzorati (her boss) what it would feel like.

They liked all of it.

I was set.

I was given a deadline.

I was excited as hell.

I was about to receive a contract when . . .

Well, I received another call from Ilena. And God, do I wish it had been about my subscription.

Ilena told me that, sadly, the *New York Times Magazine* was doing away with its Sunday serial. It had been asked to cut pages in the coming budget year, and the serial was on the chopping block. She was super-apologetic. I listened, and then tried to make Ilena feel better about the whole thing, because it wasn't her fault. I've worked at magazines and newspapers before; I knew the crushing reality of budgets.

Still, I was absolutely heartbroken.

Honestly, I was kind of inconsolable for a while.

By that time, however, I'd mentioned the serial to Marc Res-nick, my editor at St. Martin's Press, and he really dug the idea. I asked if he would mind if I wrote it anyway, making it my next book for St. Martin's Press. He agreed, and so I dove back into it. I had plotted fifteen installments, but halfway through I really loved the idea of twelve installments, one for each hour on a grandfather clock. (*Grandfather Clock* was one of the many titles I considered for this thing.) So I changed some things around. But I wrote it more or less as I'd pitched it to the *New York Times Magazine*.

If it hadn't been for Ilena and Laura, however, I really think this novel would have stayed somewhere frozen on my internal hard drive. (*Maybe it should have stayed there!* cries someone from the back row.) But I think a writer should be encouraged to do crazy things, and I'll be forever grateful to Ilena and Laura for giving me the opportunity.

BIG THANKS ARE ALSO due to my extremely patient editor, Marc Resnick, and all the good folks at St. Martin's Press—including Andrew Martin, Matthew Sharp, Sarah Lumnah, Michael Hom-ier, John Shoenfelder, Hector DeJean, and Matthew Baldacci.

Thanks to Laurence Campbell, whose illustrations adorn this book. I fell in love with Laurence's work from the moment Axel Alonso (my editor at Marvel Comics) showed me a few samples, and I've wanted to work with him ever since. I'm extremely proud to have his work in these pages.

Thanks, too, to my agent, David Hale Smith, who watched my back and held my hand the whole time, from the first pitches to Ilena, to the day it all crashed and burned, and then beyond. He spoons real nice for a Texas boy. And thanks to Shauyi Tai, his sec-ond in command.

Thanks to film agent Angela Cheng Caplan, who's been made to wait far too long for this manuscript.

Thanks to my first readers and better friends than a man deserves: Allan Guthrie, Lou Boxer, Jon Cavalier, Ed Pettit, David Thompson, and McKenna Jordan.

And last but nowhere least, thanks to my family—Meredith, Parker, and Sarah—for their patience and support during the writing of this novel.

I was in the middle of finishing *Expiration Date* when my grandfather, Louis Wojciechowski, died. I was writing this book for him. Not because it's about him, any more than it's about me. But there is a lot of him in this book, and I truly regret not putting my ass in gear and finishing this while he was still alive.

No reader should ever confuse a writer's life with his work, but I do want to make something clear:

The fictional grandfather in this novel was an imperfect man who tried his best.

My grandpop Lou was the best man I've ever known, and I miss him deeply.

ABOUT THE AUTHOR

Duane Swierczynski has written several crime thrillers for St. Martin's, including *Severance Package*, all of which have been optioned for film. He also writes the monthly X-Men series *Cable* for Marvel Comics, and has also written comics featuring Wolverine, Deadpool, the Punisher, the Immortal Iron Fist and Werewolf by Night. Most recently he's collaborated with *CSI* creator Anthony E. Zuiker on a series of thrillers called *Level 26*. He lives in Philadelphia with his wife and children. Visit him at www.duaneswierczynski.com.

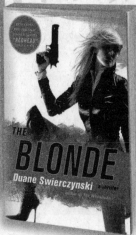